Many Rivers To Cross

Ola Opesan

Published in United Kingdom by The X Press
6 Hoxton Square, London N1 6NU
Tel: 0171 729 1199
Fax: 0171 729 1771

Printed by Caledonian International Book Manufacturing Ltd, Glasgow, UK.

Distributed in UK by Turnaround Distribution, Unit 3, Olympia Trading Estate, Coburg Road, London N22 6TZ
Tel: 0181 829 3000
Fax: 0181 881 5088

ISBN 1-874509-40-9

ABOUT THE AUTHOR

Ola Opesan lives with his wife and children in east London where he currently works as the editor of Ovation magazine. His debut noverl *Another Lonely Londoner* published in 1992 under the pseudonym Gbenga Agbenugba won him much literary praise.

CRIME TIME

Shola would probably not have stolen the police car if he was by himself. But he wasn't. Colin and Patrick were with him, on his way home from their karate class at the youth club. They were his spars — his close friends, and what was more Shola had just been bragging about what he would do to the police if he got half a chance.

He gave an exhibition of the roundhouse kick he would deliver to the head of the next policeman who tried to rough him up. After all, the cops were always harassing him. He had been stopped and searched so many times this month that he had lost count.

And now, as the three youths headed deeper into the back streets of Forest Gate, in the pouring rain with no particular place to go, a speeding police car with its sirens wailing had splashed them with muddy water from a puddle.

"Frigging bloody cops," Colin shouted after the car. "They must think this is Miami Vice or something."

Shola ran into the street and stuck his middle

finger up at the police car as it disappeared into the distance.

Though only seventeen, they had long ceased believing in the friendly neighbourhood bobby. He was a myth in their area.

"I'd like to make them pay for this," Shola fumed, staring down at his muddy jeans. "These are my favourite pair."

The three friends were still cursing the police when they got to the end of the road. When they turned the corner, they came upon the empty police car, in the middle of the road, its blue emergency lights swirling, parked outside a house with its front door wide open.

From inside the house, the angry voices of a quarrel filtered out.

Patrick was the first to react.

"Shola, here's your big chance."

He pointed to the police car keys, which were dangling from its ignition. The temptation was there waiting for them, all they had to do was act, and fast at that.

"What you saying, Shola? I'd do it if I could drive," Colin dared him.

Shola's heart was pounding. His better judgment was telling him all the reasons to just keep walking. But his friends were challenging him. Shola was no chicken. He was anything but. Everyone knew that.

"You said there's nothing more you'd love to do a few seconds ago," Patrick reminded him.

The quarrel in the house seemed to intensify as

the voices grew louder. The authoritative voice of a police officer trying in vain to calm things down. Then came the sound of broken glass. All hell broke loose after that.

The ruckus inside was the cue for Colin to make his move. He opened the back door of the car and jumped in. The next moment, Patrick had opened the front passenger door and was poised ready to get in.

"What you saying, Bro?" he grinned.

Shola put on a brave smile. "Jump in!" he said, darting towards the driver's door. Before he knew it, he was heading for trouble again.

The rest was like a nightmare.

The moment Shola turned the key in the ignition, a robust WPC emerged shouting from the house and raced towards them.

Shola, his adrenaline rushing, lost no time in reacting. He revved the engine, slipped the car into gear, slammed on the accelerator and the police car screeched away, leaving the policewoman cursing in their wake.

"Wi-i-icked!" Colin slapped Shola on the back, bubbling over with excitement.

"Yeah, spar. That was sweet," Patrick said, laughing at the figure of the policewoman hopping mad in the rain behind them. "Did you see her face? Oh boy, did you see her? She couldn't believe it. Love it!"

Shola concentrated on his driving, which was jerky to say the least. He had driven a car illegally once before but wasn't used to driving in the rain.

He didn't think to slow down as the police car skidded from one side of the road to the other. The only thing on his mind was to get away fast any which way he could.

"Where are we going?" Colin asked excitedly, this was the most fun they had had in ages.

"We can't go too far in a police car, y'know," Patrick replied.

Shola didn't care about that. They had dared him and, once again, he had risen to the challenge. "At least now you know you can't test me," he bragged.

The car's engine roared away in second gear, screaming to be shifted to third. Somewhere in the distance came the sound of a police siren. The three boys looked at each other with a mixture of fear and excitement. As the siren got closer, Shola put his foot down and increased his speed.

"Get ready," he shouted to his friends as he headed towards the junction at the bottom of the road.

Suddenly, a green van pulled out from a side street right into their path.

"What the...?!" was all Shola managed to say as he slammed on the brakes.

He might have been able to stop the car in time if it hadn't been for the rain. The brakes seemed to have little effect and the car skidded forward and slammed into the side of the van with a deafening crash.

Fortunately nobody was injured, but for a moment there was stunned silence from the passengers of the police car. The sound of the police siren getting closer shook them into action. Patrick was the first to jump out, followed quickly by Colin.

"Come on, man," Patrick called back to Shola as they made off down the street.

"Oi! Come here!" the driver of the van shouted at Shola on seeing the damage.

Shola didn't answer. Instead he abandoned the police car and tore down the road as fast as he could run, the wail of approaching sirens behind him.

He didn't know where he was running in the rain and he didn't care. Patrick and Colin had already disappeared. Now he had to get the hell out of the area, and fast. He didn't look back once. He just kept running and running and running, praying that he would have enough lung power to keep running to the end of the Earth if necessary.

That wasn't necessary. After half an hour, he slowed down. He was alone in the rain. Darkness all around him. He listened, but he couldn't hear anything. He stopped a while to regain his breath then started making his way home.

PARTY TIME

At college the next day, Shola was still buzzing from all the excitement of the night before. The summer holidays were approaching and, apart from a minor photography presentation, the crew had no more classes that term. As they sat in the main cafeteria deciding what to do for the day, Shola suggested an impromptu daytime party.

The motion was carried unanimously. The only thing left to decide was the venue. All eyes turned to Shola, since he had brought up the idea in the first place.

"But…I-I-I…" Shola tried in vain to bluff his way out of it but he was beaten into submission. "Okay, we'll have it at my place — again," he conceded, a grin spreading across his face. "But that means I don't have to chip in for booze. We've only got 'til six o'clock before my mum gets back, so we close shop at four sharp. Okay? My mum'll kill me if she finds out. I almost died last time, I'm not risking my life again."

The party was jumping. A dozen or so party people were stressing out the living room carpet which served as a dance floor. Shola was at the decks, mixing and blending. A handful of others stood by the garden door, chatting.

Shola was elated when Jackie arrived unexpectedly, but he played it cool and acted like he had not seen her. It had been like that the past month because of Jackie's insistence that she wouldn't "give it up." The "it" in question was her virginity. She was waiting for the right time. Shola had exhausted himself trying to convince her the time and the guy were right. But Jackie still wouldn't play.

Shola promised himself that he would lose *his* virginity this summer if it killed him. He had been trying without success for a year. To him, it seemed like he was the only virgin left on the planet. It was getting embarrassing.

Shola scratch-mixed deftly from one rap track with a booming bass to another. From the corner of his eye, he noticed Jackie by herself, clicking her fingers to the beat, rocking slowly. He carried on mixing and was in the process of slowing down the tempo when he felt someone tug at his sleeve. It was Jackie.

"I want a word with you," she said, motioning towards the front door.

Shola nodded. Patrick was only too glad to take over the role of DJ while Shola followed Jackie.

Outside, Jackie looked Shola over. "So we've

become strangers now, have we? Time only for polite chit-chat."

Shola chuckled to himself, pleased that she was obviously missing him. "Come, let's go to the shop," he said.

They walked slowly, exchanging only stiff pleasantries to the end of the road.

"Shola, I need to ask you something," Jackie said eventually. "Will you answer me truthfully?"

"Go on."

"I mean the absolute truth."

"Yes, I'll tell the truth… if I think it's what you want to hear."

"Shola, I want the truth even if it's not what I want to hear."

"I'll try. I'm not promising anything."

"You need to do more than just try, Shola."

"Okay, I'll try, I mean… Jackie, just get on with it. You're acting like world peace hangs on my answer."

"Okay, okay… Have you been totally faithful throughout our relationship?"

It began first as a chuckle then turned into peals of uncontrollable laughter.

"Is that it?" Shola asked, doubled up. "I thought you were going to ask me some wild, mind- blowing question."

Jackie stopped walking and glared at him. "This isn't a joke, Shola. I'm serious. I need to know."

"Okay, you're right." He pulled himself together. "You're right." He looked at her. Even with a brooding expression she looked innocent and vulnerable. Her hair, swept up into two ponytails, completed the girl-next-door look. "Yes, I've been totally faithful," he assured her. "You're the one... the only one."

"Hmm," she started walking again. "Don't be too sure about that. Your case is still under review."

Shola searched for a flicker in her eyes to tell him she was joking. Nothing. Her expression remained deadpan.

"Yes?" she casually enquired, when he continued staring at her. "Shola, there's no point giving me those looks. The jury's still out."

Shola laughed tentatively and, gradually, a grin began to spread across Jackie's lips. He was relieved.

"You had me fooled there for a minute, y'know."

"Yeah? Well you better realise that not many girls will put up with a boy who sulks 'cause he's not getting any sex."

"It wasn't that. It was..."

Jackie gave him a dubious look.

"...We've just drifted, that's all," he said, defensively.

"Yeah, but the question is, why?"

" 'Cause people drift. It happens all the time. Even to married couples."

"Oh really? Well," she began, poking him playfully in the chest, "you better remember next time we drift, there's always someone else waiting in line."

"So there's a queue, huh?" Shola laughed.

Jackie poked him in the ribs, then pinched his bum. "Alright Mr Wiseguy, have your fun while it lasts."

They stopped at the local cafe which doubled as an amusement arcade, and ordered two milkshakes. Sitting in a booth by the window, they talked freely about anything, everything and nothing in particular.

"Shola, I've been wondering..." Jackie said, "what happens when we both finish college? We won't get to see each other so often."

Shola shrugged. "I'm not really sure. You know what my plans are for the future, I want to be a DJ. I want to stay on in London and get a job at a club or on the radio. But if my father has his way, I'll be sent off to some university up north to study law or medicine."

Jackie's eyes fell to her drink.

Shola watched her absent-mindedly stir the milkshake with her straw. He took her hand.

"That's still a few months away," he said. "But no matter what happens, we'll always make time for each other. You know that."

Jackie smiled. "Sure."

Another milkshake later, Jackie decided that she had to go home. Shola walked her to the bus stop. But they could not bare to be separated yet. Each time her bus came along, neither he nor she was willing to let go of the tight embrace they were locked in and kept putting off her departure until the next bus.

Reluctantly, Jackie eventually got on a bus. Shola was standing on the curb waving goodbye when, from that very bus, stepped Florence DaCosta.

"Mum!" Shola shrieked.

Was it six o'clock already? He must have been talking to Jackie for hours. Shola could think of nothing but how his mother would skin him alive if she got home to discover a party going down.

Mrs DaCosta was so happy to see her son that she thrust her two shopping bags at him. At least she wouldn't have to carry the shopping all the way home by herself. Especially after a hard day at work.

Shola's thoughts were racing furiously. He had to think of a way to prevent her from going home. Despite, or because of, all the pressure he was under, Shola's mind went totally blank. Now when he needed a brilliant plan to save him, he could think of absolutely nothing.

"Shola, the bags will not carry themselves home," Florence reminded him in her thick West African accent as she began to make her way home.

Shola shuffled along behind his mother as she related her day. But he heard nothing, as one lame excuse after another churned through his head. By the time they turned the corner into their street, he was in a state of wild panic. If only he could delay his mother for ten minutes, he could rush on ahead and usher everybody out of the house through the back door and put the house in some sort of order. His mother however, exhausted and eager to get home to rest her weary feet, had no intention of being delayed. In fact. she increased her pace. Shola dashed ahead of her and stood in her path, bringing her to a standstill.

"Mum, did I tell you…" His mind froze.

"What? Tell me what?"

Shola's mind went blank again.

When she got no answer, Florence kissed her teeth and pushed past him. "How can you be so forgetful? Have you the memory of an old man?" she muttered and continued walking.

By now, she was a few yards from the front door. Shola scampered ahead and stood in front of the house, blocking his mother's entrance. Why, he did not know. It was all he could think of doing.

"Mum… do you fancy a drink in the pub?"

The look in his mother's eyes said it all, either she had not heard properly, or her son was going insane.

"Pub? Me?" she screwed up her face. "Have you ever seen me in a pub? Nonsense!"

Surprisingly, Shola could hear no music, no voices. He prayed for a miracle… that it was all a dream. He prayed that he hadn't woken up that morning and gone to college and invited everybody back to his place for a party.

His mum walked past him while he was praying, searching through her handbag for the house keys.

If there was such a thing as a miracle…

She turned the key in the lock.

He needed one right about…

She pushed the door open and stepped into the house.

NOW!

First there was silence. Then, "Sho-laaaaaaaaaa!"

His heart sank as he imagined the devastation before her. Why had he ever agreed to the party? Why didn't he keep an eye on the time? Why did he always have to be the one who took up any challenge? Never again. It wasn't worth it. Nothing was worth the pain that was about to follow.

"Shola. Didn't you hear me call you?"

"Yes, Mum." With heavy steps, Shola trudged into the house. "Mum, I can explain…"

"Explain? Explain how the shopping will get off the front doorstep and into the cupboards by themselves? Good. I would like to hear this."

Shola looked confused. He stepped past his mum cautiously to peep into the living room. There was no sign of a party. The place was spotless. A miracle. The only thing out of place was Patrick, sitting contentedly, watching telly with a can of shandy in his hand. Shola let out a long sigh of relief. His best friend had come through for him. One hundred percent.

"Patrick." Shola beamed, never so pleased to see his friend in all his life. His smile turned into ecstatic laughter. "Patrick! Mum, I completely forgot that Patrick was waiting for me at home. I just totally forgot. Patrick, my good friend. Patrick, my BEST friend."

Shola's mother eyed him suspiciously before making her way upstairs, muttering, "You call this forgetfulness? It is more like a disease."

As soon as she was out of earshot, Patrick assured him that everything was in order. Shola nevertheless had a quick check of the kitchen, the bathroom and the toilet. Everything was back to normal.

Suddenly, "Sho-o-o-o-o-o-o--laaaaaaaaa!"

The sound of Mrs DaCosta's voice booming from upstairs was warning enough for Patrick, who leapt from his seat, said a hurried goodbye and slipped out of the house.

Shola's mind raced. What could be wrong?

"Shola! I say, Shola-oh!"

"Yes, Mum."

"Don't give me 'yes, Mum'. Get up here and tell me who is this lying on my bed."

Shola bit his knuckles.

"Who is he? I say, *who* is he? Is he a friend of yours? Ah-ah!"

Shola climbed the stairs trying to avoid his mother's burning eyes. On the landing, he squeezed past her into the bedroom, taking care to stay out of reach of her left hand, which was as fast as a lizard's tongue. The 'devil's backhand' was how she referred to it.

Once inside the room, Shola had to prevent

himself from bursting into laughter at the sight of Richard, one of his college mates, lying drunk on the bed, his dreadlocks fanning around his face.

"So this is the type of friend you are keeping now?" Florence asked accusingly.

Shola didn't reply. He decided to get Richard out of there fast. "Come on, Rich. Let's go." He helped his friend off the bed.

"Shell." Richard was pleased to see him. "Aww, man! Where you been? Oh, my head... I feel like I've been in the ring with Tyson, man."

"Tell me later, okay? Come on. Up you get."

Shola's mother stood in the corner, clasping and unclasping her hands in disbelief. "Ah! In my room. On my bed!" she said, looking at Richard scornfully. "Shola, wait 'til your father returns from Nigeria. You think because he has travelled overseas you can get up to any kind of nonsense."

Shola avoided eye contact with his mother as he helped his friend downstairs.

"You know who's fault this is, don't you?" Richard babbled between burps. "It's Patrick's, ain't it? I told him, I don't drink lager... at least not warm lager, especially in the middle of the afternoon."

Shut up, fool, Shola wanted to scream. But he held it down.

"Oh no, Shell... I think I'm gonna throw up."

"Not in here you're not."

Shola rushed his friend out of the front door, just in time.

FATHERS AND SONS

The sound of a car door slamming and a vehicle pulling away cut through the early morning stillness. Florence DaCosta gradually surfaced from her deep sleep, unsure of what had roused her. She looked across at the digital clock on the bedside cabinet. It was still early. She knitted her brow, her eyes still weary with lack of sleep. She regretted being woken, every minute of slumber was precious before a hard day's work.

She heard the front door open and then close quietly. Florence's thoughts switched to Shola. Yesterday, she had caught him trying to sneak his record collection out of the house. She guessed he must have been invited to spin records at a party. But he was still supposed to be grounded for last week's impromptu daytime party, so she had confiscated the records and locked them away. Now, here he was sneaking home in the early hours. He must have gone to the party after all. The boy was becoming too unruly. He was too much. Quickly, she slipped into her dressing gown and rushed downstairs to catch him red-handed. She could not allow Shola to keep defying her orders, making a mockery of her attempts to discipline him.

"Ah! It is you," she gushed in surprise, as she reached the front door. "I was not expecting you 'til tomorrow."

She smoothed down her hair, slightly conscious of her 'just-out-of-bed' state and went to embrace her husband. He pushed his bulging suitcase into the living room and flopped into the armchair nearest the door.

"Ah, look at you," Florence said. "People go to Nigeria and come back exhausted, but my husband comes back looking twice as healthy."

Isaiah smiled at the compliment.

"How was the flight?"

"Tiring as usual. But the Nigeria Airways service seems to be getting better. Mind you, it could not get any worse."

"Rest small, while I make you a cup of tea."

Florence went to the kitchen to put on the kettle. After sixteen years in Britain, her husband loved his cup of tea.

With the kettle on the boil, Florence climbed the stairs to check on the twins. She opened the door to their room and looked in. Her angels were snoring gently. They looked so peaceful.

She was about to go back downstairs, when the little voice inside her head whispered, 'Florence, what about Shola? What if he defied you yet again and sneaked out of the house last night?' Gently, she opened the door to Shola's room and peeked in to discover that her fears were totally unfounded. Shola was asleep, curled up under the duvet. She was about to close the door when the little voice began again. 'Florence, what is he doing wrapped up under his quilt in the height of summer?'

With two purposeful strides she was at Shola's bedside and pulled back the duvet.

Although she half-expected it, she was still dismayed to find two plump pillows carefully laid along the length of the bed. Ah, it seemed this boy was really fond of trouble. Well, when he returned home, he would not be disappointed. For there would be plenty waiting for him now that his father was back.

Shola jogged slowly along the alley. At the party there had been plenty to drink and he had been merry. It had been a successful night. He had borrowed a friend's record collection which was almost as up-to-date as his own and, as everyone agreed, DJ Shola had really rocked the party. It had been well worth the effort. And, as a bonus, Jackie had been there too. Shola looked at his watch. His timing was spot on. He was due to get back a good five minutes before his mother's alarm clock would wake her. Everything had gone as smooth as clockwork.

In one fluid movement, he scaled the back

fence of his neighbour's garden and dropped down into his own as he had done thousands of times before. Treading carefully, he tip-toed around the range of the laser sensor that had been rigged by his father to foil any would-be burglars. Then he secured a good grip on the drainpipe that led to his bedroom window and hauled himself up. At the top, he managed to ease the window up with one hand, while gripping firmly to the drainpipe with the other. It was a dangerous exercise, but one he had perfected to an art form over the years. He swung himself onto the window ledge and tumbled headfirst into the room and onto his bed.

"Shola! What do you think you are doing?"

The shock of seeing his mother standing in the doorway paralysed him. He had been caught red-handed. What could he say?

"Florence, what's going on up there?"

When Shola heard his father's voice, he almost died.

His father appeared at the door. His mouth dropped open as he turned from the open window to Shola and back to the open window. "You...you...you..." he spluttered, pointing.

Shola braced himself for one of the best backhands in the disciplinary business.

His mother held on to her husband's arm, urging restraint.

"Leave him, don't worry yourself with him now..." she urged. "Come and get some rest. We can deal with him later. Both of us." She shot

Shola a threatening look.

Isaiah was finally placated, they left the room together. When Shola eventually managed to pick himself up, he closed his bedroom door and locked it. He switched on his stereo system and tuned into the pirate station on which he was occasionally a guest DJ. The sweet sound of soul music floated from the speakers. He felt relaxed, and lit up a butt that he had been saving. Smoking at home was an absolute no-no, but on this occasion he felt justified. He stuck his head out of the window, inhaled deeply, then let the smoke slowly drift from his lips into the crisp morning air while pondering the sentence now hanging over his head. His mother often postponed sentence to give him time to stew. The waiting was usually worse than the actual execution. But right now, he would put it out of his mind. He could see no good reason to worry himself unduly before the punishment was pronounced.

From the living room below, the excited voices of his parents floated up to Shola. It appeared his father's business trip to Nigeria, the third that year, had proved so successful, he was thinking of moving his business there permanently.

"Isaiah, I'm sure everything will be okay if we decide to return, but maybe we should give it more thought, more time to plan things," Shola heard his mother say.

"All this toing and froing, what do you think I've been doing? Yes, planning. Can't you see?

Now is the time." Mr DaCosta sounded determined. "Look, burglars in Nigeria work seven days a week. There are so many opportunities in this security alarm business, not only in the commercial sector, but also among all the private individuals swimming in this oil money. They are all so security conscious that they will jump at the chance of installing state-of-the-art equipment."

"But what about the children?"

"What about them? The twins are so young they will have no problem adjusting and Shola could do with the discipline of a Nigerian education. All this party today, party tomorrow business has got to stop. Anyway, you know we never intended to stay in this country forever."

Shola was only mildly concerned by what he overheard. His parents had discussed returning to Nigeria since as far back as he could remember, but he couldn't imagine going with them. He was a Londoner through and through, he would always be a Londoner and he had no intention of saying goodbye to his friends and all the good times to go and live in a foreign country.

Lack of sleep soon caught up with Shola and before he knew it, he was sprawled across his bed drifting off to sleep.

The very next evening Isaiah DaCosta dropped his bombshell. The family was seated at the dining table for a traditional Nigerian supper of ground rice with okra and pepper stew. Shola sat between his two younger sisters with his parents opposite. As usual Isaiah was first to finish and, with his hunger satisfied, he leaned back from the table and requested a bowl of water to wash his hands. Shola gathered together the empty plates dutifully and deposited them in the kitchen sink, before returning to the table to place the bowl in front of his father.

Isaiah dipped his fingers in the water.

"Who wants to go on holiday to Nigeria?" he asked.

"I do, Daddy," replied Gloria excitedly. She got a dig in the ribs from her twin sister for speaking with her mouth full.

Shola poured himself a drink and listened guardedly.

"Who wants to see Grandpa and Grandma?"

"Me, Daddy," was Grace's quick-fire response, as she warmed to the game.

"Daddy, are Grandma and Grandpa really, really old and wrinkly like in the pictures?" Gloria asked with a furrowed brow.

"Of course they are old. We all grow old," Florence replied.

"But sometimes I get frightened when I see the old pictures. Especially at night."

Florence looked at her daughter quizzically. "Well, if the pictures frighten you, then don't look at them anymore. Why should you be frightened of a picture?"

"Your mother and I have decided to go on holiday to Nigeria," Isaiah interrupted, "where it is hot and sunny and you can go down to the beach, build sandcastles, swim in the sea and eat lots of lollies. Would you like that?"

"Yes!" chorused the twins, before excitedly recounting some of the weird and wonderful stories they had heard about Africa.

"How long's the holiday?" enquired Shola.

"It depends."

"On what?"

"On how much you like it."

"And what if we don't?"

His father looked at him. "Why not let us get there first before you make your judgement?"

Shola remained quiet.

Isaiah continued. "There is business waiting for me to take care of in Nigeria. Your summer holiday is six weeks. Am I not right?"

Shola's mother finished her food and went to the kitchen to wash up, all the while trying to tame the excitement of the twins, who grilled her about life in Nigeria.

"When are we going?" Shola asked.

"In about three weeks from now."

"Three weeks!"

"What is the problem?"

Shola hesitated. "I'm not so sure this is going to be a holiday..."

"Are you trying to call me a liar?"

Shola knew his father's intimidatory tone was meant to deter him from his present line of questioning. But why shouldn't he have a say in what happened to him? He stood up and moved to the sofa, a safe enough distance from where he could speak his mind. "No one's calling you a liar. It's just... my friend Chas went to Trinidad on holiday and his parents kept him there."

"So what?"

"I don't want to stay in Nigeria. I like it here."

"Did anyone say you have to stay in Nigeria?"

Shola was tempted to mention the conversation he'd overheard the night before.

"Well, did they?" Isaiah demanded.

"So long as it is just a holiday," Shola muttered.

"You're calling me a liar again? Do you want me to increase your punishment to two weeks indoors with no pocket money?" Isiah shouted.

Shola shifted his frame on the sofa and switched on the TV with a well-aimed kicked.

"Shola, you better not try my patience..."

With those cautionary words, Isaiah continued to satisfy the twins' desires for more details of this mystical land called Africa.

Meanwhile Shola channel-surfed. Nothing held his attention. He turned up the volume to drown out his sisters' excited voices, without success. Anger and helplessness made his eyes glaze over. He felt isolated watching them all; one big happy family, united by the thrill of their impending holiday.

As the days passed and Isaiah DaCosta began to make plans for their trip to Nigeria, Shola began making plans of his own to leave home and find a place of his own. It was something he had considered on a few occasions, but had never really had reason until now to give it serious thought. The last time was when his father had complained about him being lazy in his studies and not helping around the house. As usual, tale after tale followed of how hard Isaiah used to work when he was young. Then he took to calling Shola 'Mr DJ' in his most derogatory tone of voice. They finally came to an arrangement whereby Shola was allowed to be 'Mr DJ' once a month, as long as he studied extra hours at home and kept his room tidy. So there was no need to leave after all. However, this time was different.

But leaving home was not as straightforward as he imagined. Where would he live? How would he survive? All his friends lived at home, it would be impossible to stay with them for more than a day or two. Jackie's place was not even worth considering. Her strict God-fearing Caribbean parents weren't even aware she had a boyfriend. All hell would break loose if they discovered him in her bedroom.

Shola racked his brains, but found no solution. Even sleeping rough seemed more desirable to him now than being tricked into going to live in Nigeria. He lay on his bed looking out at the darkening summer sky, regretful that he still had three days left to serve of his curfew. Life seemed so much sweeter in the summer, why couldn't it be like this all year round? But that was not reason enough for him to want to leave London and his friends. This was his whole life. The only life he knew.

UPROOTED

Shola still couldn't believe it was really happening. But it was. The plane tickets had been bought and the suitcases were all packed for the trip to Nigeria. Shola had still not decided whether he was going to be on that flight or not, yet here he was, on what was possibly his last evening in London at the cinema with Jackie, but lumbered with an uncle from France. Shola's parents' house was to be left in his care whilst they were away.

His uncle had held fast to Shola's long-forgotten promise to take him sightseeing the next time he was in London. The fact that Shola wanted to spend some quality time with Jackie, was of no concern to his uncle. A promise was a promise.

Shola found it hard to concentrate on the film. Jackie sensed Shola's unease and snuggled close with her head on his shoulder.

After the film they escorted Shola's uncle

home, then departed quickly. It was getting dark as Shola and Jackie strolled the streets aimlessly. It was a pleasant evening and now that they were alone together, they were in no hurry.

"Do you really think your parents will stop you coming back?" Jackie asked, breaking the silence.

Shola didn't know. He felt like a sheep being dragged with the flock, unable to change direction or affect his own destiny.

"There must be a way we can sort this out so you can stay," Jackie said. Her voice cracked, betraying her emotions.

"I don't know. My head's at melting point from thinking so hard. All I know is, if I go to Nigeria, I'm not staying there. I'll be back a lot sooner than you think. That's a promise." Shola was trying to reassure himself as much as Jackie.

"What type of ticket did your dad buy, single or return?"

Shola shrugged his shoulders. "He won't show it to me."

They walked on in silence. The last thing Shola wanted was for the night to turn into a long goodbye. He didn't want to get too sentimental, but if this was to be their last night, he wanted it to be special. And there was one thing that would guarantee it would be special. It was now or never.

"Jackie, can I be truthful and tell you what's on my mind?"

"What is?"

"Sex."

Jackie stopped. She took a closer look at Shola and realised he was serious.

"I think I'll just ignore that," she said, sashaying past him. "Anyway, how come you've suddenly gone crazy over sex?"

"Jackie, do you know what it's like going to bed with your hormones running crazy all day long?"

"Should I?"

"Well, let me tell you, it aches all day."

Jackie laughed softly.

"You know all those stories we guys tell each other? It's the living porkies. The closest most of us get to sex is seeing frilly knickers on TV ads. And that includes me."

Jackie burst into laughter. "Shola, you're crazy."

"I think you're right."

They reached a deserted bus shelter where they decided to stop for a while.

"Is this little sob story supposed to soften me up so you can have your wicked way with me before you go?" Jackie queried, teasingly.

"I'm just telling you the truth. You like the truth don't you? Straight up, that's what's on my mind, sex. Thing is, it takes two."

"It does?"

"Yep. Me and you."

"Oh really? I don't know about that..."

"Well, you and I then."

Jackie laughed. "Come here. You're raw, but...

kinda fresh too." She pulled him close for a marathon french kiss.

Whatever Shola was feeling for Jackie before, he felt it a hundred times more now. It was as if he had been kissed for the very first time. How could one kiss feel so good? It felt as if he had been lifted clean off his feet and, as they embraced, he wished it would never end. Before the kiss was over, Shola had decided that he would not, under any condition, be going to Nigeria. He couldn't bear being so far away from Jackie.

The kiss had a similar effect on Jackie also. Even as they embraced she knew that tonight was the night she had spent so much time daydreaming of. Tonight, she decided, she would become a woman.

The phone rang the moment Shola got home that night.

It was Patrick calling from a call box, his voice thick with panic.

"They've got Colin," he cried. "I saw them."

"Slow down," Shola said. "Who's got Colin?"

"The cops, man. The cops."

Suddenly Shola understood what Patrick was talking about. He had completely forgotten about the joyride in the police car. He assumed they had gotten away with it. They hadn't heard anything.

"Are you sure it's about the car?"

"What else could it be?" Patrick said, more

urgently. "We've got to think of something and think of something fast."

But that was the problem, Shola couldn't think of anything that would help Patrick. His mind was already thousands of miles away, on a beach in Nigeria…

"Listen, Shell, I have to hurry 'cause my money's gonna finish. But I just want you to know, I'm your friend and I'll never grass on you. And Colin won't either."

Somehow Shola couldn't see that. He was the one who had stolen the police car. The other two were just passengers. The police wouldn't let the case drop until they had caught the main villain. The more he thought about it, the more Nigeria didn't seem like such a bad option.

"Hear wha', Shola, money's finished. I gone."

"Try and lie low," Shola advised.

"Hey, you know me…" was all he managed to say before the call line went dead.

Now Shola began to panic. For all he knew, the police were on their way to his house right now. He climbed the stairs up to his bedroom and locked the door. He opened his window and listened for the sound of a car pulling up. But there was none. He was still unable to relax.

If the police arrived tonight, he decided, he would climb out of the window and run away. He lay on his bed turning things over and over in his head until, eventually, he fell into a deep sleep.

*   *   *

It was only five o'clock yet the sun's light was already pushing back the darkness. Shola sat in the back seat, it still seemed like a dream. Today was the day. He was leaving London indefinitely. His mother made a few final checks on the house before climbing into the car. Shola's uncle switched on the engine and pulled away from the kerb. As the car rolled steadily down the road, Shola turned for a final glance at their house just as a police car pulled up outside and two uniformed officers climbed out. Shola could feel his heart thumping as he held his breath, hoping that his uncle didn't look in his rearview mirror. Suddenly, Heathrow airport seemed so far away.

A WHOLE NEW WORLD

Dear Shola,
I hope you can see and read the words I'm writing, as my hands are shaking in anger while my tears stain the page. You haven't even reached the airport yet and my heart already feels the pain of having been torn from your side.

Why did your parents do this to us? My mum saw me crying earlier and all she could say is 'The pain will ease with time'. What the hell does she know, she's been with my dad all her life.

I don't know why, but I can't stop crying, the more I wipe away the tears is the more they flow. I can't believe that from now on our only contact will be by letter. No more quick phone calls, no more secret meetings, just letters.

Shola, the only thing that can bring a smile to my face at the moment is my last memory of being with you. Thank you for making it so special. I know I've always made a big fuss about 'giving it up' but now I'm glad that I did. When I close my eyes I see you so clearly, I can almost feel your touch. My whole body tingles just to think of what we did together. Up until now I have always thought that I would feel guilty about losing my virginity before I was married but, Shola, I'm so glad it was to you.

I know we never really discussed our true feelings, even though you're always telling me how much you check for me. When you told me last night that you love me, I wasn't sure if you meant it. I know you'll think me cruel for saying this, but I thought you only said it so that you could get into my knickers.

Now that you're away from me the question's no longer just whether you love me or not, but whether our love can withstand the pressure and added strain of the distance between us. From where I am sitting in London, Africa feels like it is all the way on the other side of the world.

Shola, the only regret I have about sleeping with you is the fact that we're going to have to wait for the longest while before we can do it again. And, by the way, there's no need to worry about me meeting anyone else, after sharing such a special part of my life with you I don't want anybody else in my life.

Shola, I must tell you, I know you made me promise not to come to your house before you left for the airport but I couldn't help myself. I just wanted to hug you one more time, but I got there too late. You were being driven away in your uncle's car as I arrived. I sobbed my heart out, wishing I had got there five minutes earlier. While I stood watching your empty house with memories flashing through my mind, a police car pulled up and broke my train of thought. When I bumped into Patrick later, he gave me a run down of the trouble you got into the other night. I can't think what possessed you to do such a foolish thing and think you'd get away with it.

Well, consider yourself lucky, you left

for Nigeria in the nick of time. Colin and Patrick got arrested and the police are now awaiting your return.

Oh damn, I'm going to have to end here as I've just heard my mum come through the door and I haven't washed the dishes. She doesn't care that I'm distressed over losing you ('cause that's what it feels like — as if you've gone for a lifetime not for a few months). All she cares about is church, she keeps telling me leave it to God. I hope she's right.

Goodbye my love, answer as soon as you receive my letter. I love you with all my heart.
Jackie xxx

Shola trailed after his parents and sisters from the plane to the customs and immigration checkpoint, peeling off layers of clothing as he went.

He leaned against a wall, waiting for his parents to complete the formalities, fanning himself with a magazine. Even though he was finally in the Federal Republic of Nigeria, it all still seemed to be a dream.

He followed his parents into the crowded baggage hall at Murtala Muhammed International. The sea of glistening black faces reminded him of carnival time in London.

Two baggage collectors, one in flip-flops the other barefooted, rushed up with their rickety trolleys to solicit trade from Shola's parents, who soon gave in to the fast-talking operators. After a short wait they had all their luggage loaded onto the trolleys and were making their way through.

They emerged into the air-conditioned Arrivals Hall to be confronted by a teeming crowd. Isaiah stood on tiptoe trying to spot his father, who had promised to meet them there, amongst the other excited faces waiting expectantly for friends and relatives to arrive from overseas.

Shola's images of Africa were being shattered one by one. The airport, to his surprise, had more modern facilities than he had expected; neon signs, lifts and automatic sliding doors, which was in contrast to the thin layer of dust apparent on every surface of the building's interior. On the floor, the dust accumulated into gritty sand which was thick enough to show footprints.

Isaiah huddled the family into a corner, paid off the baggage collectors and went in search of his father.

A tall man in a light green safari suit walked through the automatic doors and Shola immediately recognised his grandfather, though he looked slightly older than the photos he had seen.

Papa DaCosta was the third generation of freed slaves who had made their way back to

Freetown from Brazil, and from there on to Nigeria where they set up a homestead in Yaba. A retired lawyer, he was a tall, gangly man, with a slight stoop.

Shola inched forward to greet him. It seemed the ancients were right in saying 'you can smell your blood', for the minute Shola's grandfather turned and caught sight of his only grandson, a smile widened across his face.

The family followed Papa DaCosta to his waiting car in the airport car park and he drove them home to his place in Yaba. There was a lot of catching up to do from all sides. Papa DaCosta made sure that each of his grandchildren gave him a full run down on how they were doing with their education and on their life in London. For the next few days, all the family did was talk, as one member of their extended family after another popped in to make the acquaintances of the relatives they had never met. Shola especially was popular amongst all his cousins.

> Dear Shola,
> I hope when you receive this letter you are in good health.
>
> I'm assuming you've been ill (literally on your deathbed) and that is why you haven't replied as yet, or didn't you receive my letter?

I'm not feeling too good myself, I've had the last three days off college, it must be something I've eaten. For the last two days as I've laid in bed I tell myself that today's the day that your letter will arrive in the post.

But you know what, I don't care. I'm missing you so badly, I need to hold you, feel your hands on my bare skin. This past fortnight without you have been sheer hell. I can't seem to sleep, I don't want to eat and you're constantly on my mind. I can't wait to get your letter to let me know how much longer we must be apart ?

Oh, the guys said to 'big you up', Richard is well chuffed, he managed to get himself a summer job with the chance of some part time hours during term time.

I heard on the grapevine that Patrick's girlfriend left him over this last incident with the police because she said he's wotless and he'll never amount to anything. A bit harsh, don't you think? Judging by Patrick's face, when I saw him, it's not just a rumour either.

I haven't seen much of Colin though,

his short stint in a police cell seems to have put him on the straight and narrow. He has decided to buckle down to studying. He's even asked if he could recruit my help during the holiday. Don't fret (I know what you must be thinking), I shall rebuke all his advances if he decides to get fresh (Joke)!!

Shola, the only other reason I can think of for your not answering my letter is that you're so distressed you can't put pen to paper. I can't bare to think of you like that, so please answer this letter and put me out of my misery.
Missing you bad. Jackie xxx

Shola had been in Nigeria two weeks and not for one moment had he thought of asking his father when they were going to return to London. Literally and metaphorically, he had been thrust into a new world and a fresh experience. It was as if he was seeing life through someone else's eyes. But this wasn't a documentary on Africa. This wasn't Tarzan or Indiana Jones. He had not come across any gullible natives. If anyone was being taken for a ride, it was him, in the colourful, erratic, smoggy, crowded rush of life in the metropolis of Lagos. This was real. He was live and direct in Africa.

Shola's grandparents had offered them two large rooms to stay in. Florence and Isaiah occupied the larger room, leaving the room overlooking the stream behind the house to Shola and his sisters.

He felt inconvenienced having to share and couldn't help feeling resentful towards the high-spirited twins, even though he knew it was not their fault. He hadn't felt this way towards them since they were babies. Back then, he often wondered why his parents left it so late to have more children. Why had they let him get used to almost eleven years of undivided love and attention, before conceiving his sisters to invade his space? He had previously known a privileged life, a life in which all his needs and wants were catered for. He had always been the first to parade the latest fashion in school. He was envied by, but not envious of, his friends who all had siblings and only received new clothes and presents for christmas or birthdays. Until the arrival of his sisters, every weekend was like a birthday to Shola.

Now Shola was having an excellent time in Lagos and meeting new people every day. He had managed to enrol on a class taken by the best karate teacher in Lagos and was improving his martial arts skills by the day.

At first he thought the language would be a problem but everyone seemed to speak pidgen English, he even began to learn a few words himself.

The heat took a little getting used to though, that and the mosquitos were Shola's main problems. At first Shola found himself sleeping every afternoon. Sometimes as long as two to three hours because the blazing sun sapped his energy. But he made up for the lost time during his waking hours.

A lot of his time was spent chasing his grandparents' sixteen year old housegirl. He followed her on every errand: to the market with its numerous rows of open stalls and freshly displayed farm produce and to the bakery. He even accompanied her on her lonely jaunts to the railway tracks where she met up with her friends, who were also housegirls or houseboys, to catch up on the neighbourhood gossip.

It was on one of these journeys with the housegirl that Shola decided to practice the art of 'hanging on', as he had seen many young bus conductors and Lagos commuters do from the overcrowded VW combi buses. 'Hanging on', literally involved being suspended from the vehicle with your feet on the tailgate.

Shola was 'hanging on', and enjoying the buzz from the wind rushing into his face. As he had thought, it was as easy as taking candy from a baby. He winked at the bus conductor, who smiled back. But then the driver of the vehicle started racing another mini-bus. The vehicles moved so close together that Shola had visions of being crushed. He was now 'hanging on' for dear life and screaming at the driver to slow down.

The conductor couldn't help chuckling loudly at his passenger's anxiety.

Shola did try to get a summer job, but soon gave up. The closest he came to anything was securing an application form. He slowly came to realise that in Nigeria, you had to be well-connected before you even stood a chance of applying for a job.

Shola had not even sniffed an interview, until a friend of the family's came to the rescue, putting him on to her uncle who would try to get him a clerical vacancy at the local Water Corporation.

On the morning of the interview, Shola left home full of enthusiasm and expectation. His first obstacle on arriving at the Water Corporation's offices was to get past the gate man. He tried using his contact's name to get into the building, but the gate man insisted that he knew all the VIPs who worked there and the name Shola mentioned was not one of them.

"Then there's the little matter of your foot tax," the gate man told him with a smirk.

Shola knew that if he didn't oblige, he could forget entering the building, so against his principles, he gave the gate man some small change and gained entrance. On arrival at the personnel office, Shola approached the desk of the receptionist who was engrossed in a lifestyle magazine.

"Excuse me..."

Turning the page, she raised an enquiring eye.

"Can I help you?" she asked, in a tone that really said, 'What the hell do you want? Can't you see I'm busy?'

When Shola stated his business, she motioned to him to take a seat, like he was some irritant fly that had landed on her desk, then returned to her magazine, constantly twiddling the loose ends of her plaits with her stained fingers. Every now and then a guffaw exploded from her purple painted lips.

Shola waited patiently and calmly.

The receptionist finished reading her magazine, arranged her desk and beckoned Shola over. She handed him an application form, which he quickly filled in. He was then told to take it to the manager's secretary. He entered the ante-office, greeted the male secretary and was told to take a seat next to five other hopefuls. Shola wondered how many job vacancies were available. This was serious competition. Meanwhile, peels of laughter emanated from inside the manager's office at regular intervals.

After a short while of waiting, the manager's secretary called Shola outside into the passage, guiding him away from the door.

"Have you my small something?" he asked, in a hushed voice.

"Small something?" Shola echoed.

"Ah, do I have to spell it out? One hundred naira."

He had to pay yet another bribe. Shola suppressed his growing rage at the corruption that plagued every level of business in Nigeria, and decided to bargain with the secretary.

"I will pay you your a hundred naira," he began, "but only after I have seen the manager."

The secretary pondered his offer for a while. "Hmm. Okay," he agreed, reluctantly, before returning to his office.

Another applicant, a tall lady with sunglasses entered to submit her form. The laughter from the manager's office spilled out as the door was opened by a short, yellow man who Shola took an immediate dislike to.

The man ushered his visitors out then turned to the people waiting outside his office.

"I am the manager," he announced and enquired about everyone's business.

Like an army roll call, each applicant stated their business and the name of the person who had referred them. Shola added that he was qualified to excel at the post. The manager let out an amused sigh before calling the woman who had been last to arrive into his office and a short while later, his raucous laugh could be heard, followed by a tentative giggle from the woman.

The secretary called Shola outside again. This time he insisted on getting his fee. With much bargaining, Shola got him to accept half the fee, for the present.

As they re-entered the office they bumped into the manager who was leaving in a hurry with the woman interviewee. The secretary then informed everyone that the manager had gone to lunch.

Shola returned after lunch and resumed his waiting, telling himself to keep cool, and maybe he would get his due reward. Forty five minutes later, the manager returned to his office to inform everybody that the last vacancy had just been filled. Shola felt an uncontrollable rage rise up within him. He had wasted his whole day.

"You!" he called to the secretary. "Give me my money back."

The secretary did not even deny receiving money from him. He let out a small chuckle. "I think you misunderstand," he started. "That was an administration fee. It is non-refundable."

"What? That money was a bribe and you know it. I want my money. Now!" Shola demanded, stepping up to the secretary.

The manager stood by, watching amused.

"Ah-ah! What is wrong with you?" the secretary wailed.

"Now!" Shola demanded, slamming his fist on the desk.

The secretary tried to laugh it off, but his laughter was hollow and tinged with embarrassment. He lowered his eyes from Shola's steely glare, dipped his hand in his pocket and pulled out a slim wad of notes, proceeding to peel off a one hundred naira note. Shola snatched the wad and began distributing hundred naira notes to each of the other disappointed applicants.

"Eh, what do you think you are doing?" the secretary jumped over his desk to retrieve the money.

But Shola shoved him away with one hand. He pocketed his money, and threw the remaining notes on the table then headed for the door.

"Young man..." the manager called.

Shola turned, levelling his gaze at him.

"...There is no need to act like that."

"Is that all you have to say?" Shola sneered.

"Don't raise your voice at me, young man. Who do you think you are talking to?"

Shola bit his tongue to stop a stream of obscenities leaving his mouth. Nevertheless, "Wanker!" escaped underneath his breath.

"Wanker!" the manager exclaimed in wonderment. "Wanker you too!"

The astounded job seekers watched with mouths agape as Shola left the room. He passed the receptionist, who called to him to sign out, but he held up his middle finger to her. At the gate, the security guard was lighting a cigarette. He paused to ask, "Oga, anything for me?"

Shola couldn't believe his ears. He marched up to the booth and snatched the cigarette from the guard's lips, just praying for the guard to say one word in protest. He didn't make a sound.

As he made his way home, Shola wondered what the future held for Nigeria. How many enthusiastic Nigerian youths had been driven to despair because they had no connections among the elite class? He so badly wanted to challenge the status quo, but he knew he was not in a position to do so.

CONGRATULATIONS

With no hope of getting a job, the National Stadium close to his grandparents' house became one of Shola's regular haunts. He spent a lot of time hanging around its several sports complexes; the tennis arena, swimming pool, football grounds, volleyball and basketball courts.

One activity that caught Shola's imagination was the improvised sport of skateboarding down the long twisting ramp that led into the main stadium — the home of the national football team.

He soon excelled in his new hobby, winning many friends and admirers with his antics — almost as many as with his English accent. It didn't take him long to realise that this difference between him and the Nigerian boys was particularly attractive to the ladies, and he was fast learning to handle all the attention he was getting.

It was under a darkening sky, behind the swimming pool, in the tall grass that grew wild and free, that Shola had his first intimate experience with a beautiful Nigerian girl in the form of a young swimming coach with a shapely body.

From the moment Shola discovered the fruits of the garden, he couldn't wait for the evenings when he would meet up with his dream lover at the National Stadium.

When his parents furniture arrived from London by sea, it initially set alarm bells ringing in Shola's head. But he was too seduced by the sultry sun and the affections of his love goddess to think of questioning his father about going back to London. He was having too much fun to remind himself about Jackie or the police back home.

As far as Shola was concerned, Nigeria was now his home. He was having more fun than he had thought possible and he wasn't about to return in a hurry to Europe where all that waited for him was police trouble.

His exam results arrived from London at the end of the summer and fortunately he had passed.

His A-Level grades were good enough for him to get on an Economics undergraduate course at the University of Lagos, a decision he was not at all adverse to, especially since he had heard learned that some of the most beautiful women in Nigeria studied there. Shola was looking forward to making the acquaintances of them all. But first, he had to write to Jackie. She had written so many letters now that he could no longer delay sending her one in reply.

What's happening, baby?
Firstly let me say sorry for taking so long to reply to your letters, I hope you can forgive me, there's been a lot going down.

The heat takes a little getting used to, I spend a lot of my time sleeping. I've tried to get myself a summer job but failed, that's a long story. All I'll say on that subject is, they say the English are shrewd, but my fellow Africans do not miss a trick!

My time away from you has given me space to think, not that you didn't give me that before, but away from the hustle and bustle of everyday life in London I now realise what I really want to do and have decided to stay on here and complete my university studies.

Don't think that we won't see each other, I will find ways and means of getting money to buy a ticket for you to fly out here and spend your vacations with me.

Jackie, this is where I end, my mum is calling me for dinner (boy have I missed her cooking) and, as always, I've got a lot of housework to do afterwards.

Tell the guys that I'm okay and that I've been very busy, but that I'll drop them all a line soon.
Til we meet again. Shola xxx

Fresher's Week was a good opportunity for Shola to size up the female talent at the university. He had made a mental note of five or six 'potential partners' for the year.

Shola quickly made friends with several of the male students. He was popular, not least for his English accent which everybody seemed to find very amusing and Shola was often called upon by his fellow undergraduates to recount stories from London. In fact, Shola was enjoying university life so much that the last thing on his mind was academic work and he totally forgot about London, the police, Colin, Patrick and Jackie.

Dear Shola,
I don't know how to say this, I can't think of any way to soften the blow so I'll just get straight to the point. This

morning I found out that I am definitely pregnant.

Shola, this is a nightmare, what the hell am I going to do? With you thousands of miles away I've got no one I can turn to. I can't even begin to think of telling my parents — my mum will freak and my dad is bound to disown me. I can hear him now, 'You've brought shame to the family'. To be honest, Shola, I don't even know if I want to keep it, I'm too young to be tied down.

I'm still in a state of shock, I only went to the doctor for a check-up. It wasn't food poisoning as I thought, it was morning sickness that I was suffering.

I'm at my wits end. This is the biggest decision of my life and I have to make it on my own. I just wish you were here to help me to decide the right thing to do. Right now as I write these words to you I'm racking my brain as to when and how to tell my parents or, indeed, whether I need to tell them. If I decide not to keep it then there would be no point in distressing them with my news.

This isn't the way I imagined it to be, Shola. This isn't the way I had planned my life. Even now, when I think of the future, I think of spending the rest of my life with you. But the longer you are away in Nigeria, the more uncertain I am as to what the future holds for us both.

I feel like screaming, I'm so alone and afraid. It's scary to think my whole life depends on whatever decision I make now. Shola, if you can get to a phone, please call me as we need to discuss this matter urgently. If not please, please, please reply to this letter immediately.

I'm so confused, please help me Shola.
Love Jackie xxx

ROOTS

If he had major worries on his mind, Shola wasn't showing it. On his return home after the first few weeks at university, he was looking forward to spending time with his family, relaxing from the cycle of studying hard and playing hard. He had attended every sort of party possible in his first semester at the University of Lagos: beach parties, room parties, tea parties, early morning parties, late evening parties, midday parties, pool parties, discos and clubs. Shola had seen it all.

It was his first visit to the family's new house. It was sparsely furnished, but the important thing for him was that it had three bedrooms, which meant he no longer had to share with his sisters. What's more, in the living room there was a VCR, TV and recliner, three good reasons why he should try and spend more time at home.

Shola hadn't been home long, before the twins came running in from the sweltering yard where they had been playing a game of tag. They threw themselves at their brother. Shola scooped them up in a tight embrace and smothered them with hugs, kisses and tickles. Time apart had made him grow more fond of his sisters. They seemed to have grown so much in the few weeks he had been away, it was amazing.

The twins began firing questions breathlessly. What is university like? How many people in each class? Had he made any friends? What about girlfriends? Shola answered all their questions as he unpacked.

There was something different about the way his sisters spoke. They had adapted to life in Nigeria so rapidly that they were now sounding like they were born and bred in Lagos.

"Mosquitoes bit me," Grace said proudly.

"Didn't Daddy get you mosquito nets?"

"Yes, he has, Brother Shola," Gloria answered.

"Mummy says the mosquitoes like our blood," chimed Grace. "But as long as we don't pick the the bite marks, they will go away. Brother Shola, Grace always picks hers."

"Brother Shola, that's not true. She..."

"Whoa! Time out. What's with the 'Brother Shola' business? Why are you calling me that?"

"Mummy and Daddy said we should call anyone older than us 'brother' or 'sister'. That's the way people do in Nigeria."

"Well, that's fine. You can call everyone else 'brother' or 'sister'. But we already know I'm your brother, so let's stick with just Shola."

"Okay, Broth... I mean, Shola."

Shola couldn't help smiling as he gently tugged the long plaits that covered Grace's head. Suddenly, she shouted "I'm it!" and Gloria almost fell over herself trying to run out of the room, to put some vital yards between herself and Grace.

Shola lay on his bed and began to read yet another letter from Jackie, He was unsure of whether to reply. He didn't know what to say. What could he say after the news of her pregnancy? How could he possibly tell her that something had been lost between them, that happiness does not make the heart grow fonder, that he didn't feel the same way about her as he had felt when he was in London? He was to become a father, but it didn't feel like it at all. London was so far away that, to Shola, his world there belonged to another lifetime. If only he could erase certain things from that life, like the one and only passionate night he and Jackie spent together.

He read the letter again. Jackie expressed how much she missed him. Shola wished he could say the same, but he couldn't.

Shola's idea of playing happy families that weekend soon disappeared when he saw his mother later that evening. She was sitting in the recliner with her arms folded across her chest. Even the 'terrible twosome', as he referred to the twins, appeared subdued.

Shola's mind seized on the worst scenario as he walked into the room and took a seat opposite his mother.

"Mum, what's wrong? Has anything happened? Where's Dad?" he asked, deeply concerned.

His mother shrugged her shoulders. The twins began whispering amongst themselves. Florence cast a look in their direction and told them to go outside and play. The twins were reluctant at first but hurried out of the room on receiving a reassuring signal from Shola. He then learned that his father had been away for three days.

"With no word?"

"Nothing," Florence replied, resignedly.

"Have you called the police?"

"No. This is not the first time. He has done this several times before. He doesn't even bother to call his parents' home and leave a message to reach us."

"So you're left to worry?"

Florence nodded.

Shola had been aware for a while that his family were experiencing financial difficulties. Moving the whole family back to Nigeria had cost a lot more than was initially anticipated and his father was having to work day and night to keep the security systems business afloat. They were even being forced to sell their house in London cheaply for a quick sale, just to save the business. His mother was against it. To her it represented the burning of the final bridge, but she had yielded to her husband's request that it was their one last chance to salvage the business.

The business had suffered from the perennial problem of cashflow. Mainly caused by some debtors pleading poverty, while others blatantly refused to accept that they owed any money. Even getting money from the big companies proved very slow, with staff demanding backhanders before doing the job they were paid to carry out. To deny these key personnel their 'gift' was to delay for months — sometimes years — the payment of invoices. Isaiah DaCosta had at yet not got to grips with the Nigerian way of doing business, he was now in financial trouble.

"I don't understand how he can just disappear like this?" Shola said.

"My son, you know your father is a very proud man. He says it is up to him to look after his family. But sometimes, in this Nigeria of ours, it becomes too..." her voice faltered as she choked back her sobs "...too hard."

Shola cast his eyes to the ground, unable to bear seeing his mother cry. She was a strong woman. This was the first time he had seen her in such a state.

Late that night, as Shola kept his mother company at home, Isaiah DaCosta burst through the front door, drunk. Dragging himself to the settee, he collapsed in it.

"Has that Mr Landlord been here for his money?" he sneered, slurring his words. He produced a nylon bag. "Well, here it is," he said, flinging it across the room. Isaiah lay stretched out on the settee, his eyes closed, a content smile fixed on his face.

Shola looked at his mother, who just shook her head, got up and left the room.

"Shola, are you there?"

"Yes, Dad."

Isaiah said nothing more. Within seconds he had fallen into a deep sleep.

Shola sat staring at him. It hurt him so much to see his father so heavily inebriated. After a while, he stood up to leave, but first he gently removed his father's shoes and socks. Then he tip-toed out of the room, closing the door softly behind him.

BIG MAN ON CAMPUS

It was five minutes past midnight. The night was warm with a slight breeze. To the uninitiated it would seem like the Moremi Hall car park was where the party was at. The female students were pouring out of its gates in the finest, latest, Milan, New York and Paris fashions. A steady flow of saloon cars were pulling in or driving out, their stereos pumping the latest tunes. The street traders were trading, the suya was roasting on an open grill and everyone was dressed for a party.

Abi, Shola's room mate, sat in the driver's seat of the VW convertible. He was Professor Uwe's son and had invited Shola to stay with him in the staff quarters at the end of his first semester. Tonight's party was to be the last serious jam before they settled down to study for their exams.

Shola checked his appearance in the wing mirror as a red Mercedes convertible pulled into the car park, two spaces from Abi's VW, with its stereo thumping. The tinted electric windows glided down to reveal a young man with a confident smile. Abi immediately recognised Prince Johnson, one of the patrons of the Elite club, who busied himself, hugging and calling out to his many female admirers.

Shola meanwhile had spotted Evelyn, his date for the night. She was the reigning Miss Moremi Hall and had intelligence to go with her beauty. As she approached, Shola climbed out of the car to greet and admire her. He couldn't resist planting a huge kiss on her lips.

The only person they were waiting for now was Abi's girlfriend. Evelyn agreed to go up to her halls to hurry her along.

An hour later, Shola and Abi were still waiting in the car park for Evelyn to come back from her mission. It was nearly one in the morning and the air had stilled. Abi was tired of waiting and so was Shola, since it wasn't even his girl he was waiting for. When Evelyn finally returned, she brought bad news.

"She's not coming."

Abi sat bolt upright. "What?"

"You must be joking!" Shola chorused.

Evelyn put her hands on her hips and gave him a 'Do I look like I'm laughing?' look.

"Why not?" Abi asked.

"She wouldn't say. She just said I must tell Shola sorry for keeping him waiting."

"Tell Shola? What about me?"

Abi got out of the car and slammed the door, fuming. He made straight for the main entrance to the girls' accommodation block.

Shola caught up with Abi in time to convince him that the security guards would overpower him should he attempt to enter Moremi Hall at this hour. It was a women only residence.

Abi was nevertheless determined to gain access. In which case, he would have to scale the fence around the back. That sounded like a challenge to Shola and he couldn't resist. Having scaled the fence many times before, Shola was confident and led the way.

They made their way along the corridor towards Joy's room, under the disapproving glares of the scantily clad female inhabitants of the block who sat outside their dormitories chatting.

Abi burst into his girlfriend's room without knocking and immediately had cause to regret it, as Joy's room mate, who had been lying topless on the top bunk of the bed, screamed before fleeing out of the room covering her naked breasts as best she could.

Seconds later, Joy stepped out onto the landing, gearing up to scold Abi. Then she caught sight of Shola, who returned her smile with a wink. After a full ten minutes of arguing, Abi was finally able to elicit Joy's objection to going to the party. It was payback for Abi's neglect of her at the last party they had attended. Shola tried not to laugh as she dredged up the past. Abi apologised profusely. Eventually Joy accepted his apologies and agreed to be outside within twenty minutes.

Abi and Shola began making their way back to the car. As they hit the third floor landing, they were confronted with Joy's room mate, dressed in a borrowed T shirt, with two security guards in tow.

Abi and Shola turned and sprinted in the opposite direction. The security guards gave chase.

They descended a flight of stairs, to the second floor and were approaching the first, when they were confronted by another set of guards coming up the stairs. As the security guards closed in on them drawing their nightsticks, Abi and Shola launched themselves instinctively over the banister and fled down the stairs. They kept running until they had scaled the fence again and landed safely on the other side. Out of breath, they supported each other, and burst out laughing. That was the most fun they had had all day.

"Did you see that big fat security guard try and outrun me? He's going to have to get down to the gym and work out some more if he's going to stand a chance of taking on King Shola, the one hundred metre champ of the University of Lagos."

"If you're the champ, how comes I was ahead of you?" Abi protested.

"That's because you were more afraid of the security guards than I was," Shola laughed.

Such was university life for Shola. There

seemed to be an exciting adventure around every corner he turned, and a close shave up ahead awaiting.

Abi had taken the place of Colin and Patrick in Shola's life. Just like them, he knew what made Shola tick and they shared the same views on almost everything. Now, the two were rarely separated at university and had begun to get a name for themselves amongst the students as a team. You could not invite Shola somewhere without inviting Abi and vice versa.By the same token, if you took a dislike to one you could hardly befriend the other. They were two peas in a pod. Neither was it altogether clear who influenced who the most in the relationship. Certainly, Abi was Shola's guide through Nigerian student etiquette, but many of their fellow students had begun to notice how Abi now spoke English with something of a London twang.

THINGS FALL APART

Like most of his mates Shola had a lot of work to catch up with before the exams and decided he was better off working at home during the one week study break. He had worked out a study plan that enabled him to pace himself and keep his workload in perspective. This made him feel good.

It was one of those rare Sundays when Isaiah had accompanied Florence and the twins to church. Florence had been born into Catholicism, but marriage to Isaiah had brought her into the Anglican faith. Now she moved between the two. And to add to her blessings, she occasionally attended a friend's Pentecostal fellowship on Wednesday evenings.

Like many Nigerians, Florence felt the sharp divide between the very rich and the very poor, to be found in modern African society. The DaCostas could not yet be classified as poor, but their standard of living was declining by the day.

It was now nearly four months since their return to Nigeria and the security business was still not bringing in any money. The anxiety of struggling to provide basic needs for her family had driven Florence to seek God with a new fervour.

On his own in the house, Shola felt bold enough to roll up a spliff. Indian hemp, as it was known, was his only vice. He decided a few puffs would be sufficient and then he'd get back to his studies. But the herb mellowed his senses so much, he decided he'd earned a break until the afternoon. He moved from the desk to his bed, where he took his time finishing his spliff, before drifting off to sleep.

By 11.15am the family's rickety Toyota had pulled into the street in which they lived. Shola's father stopped at the local tyre shop, ostensibly to collect a spare tyre and suggested that his wife and children walk the short distance home, rather than wait for him to take care of business. Florence knew full well that the tyre shop doubled as a liquor store and that her husband's real business was to exchange his crate of empty beer bottles for a crate of full ones, but she took the children's hands and led them home.

Grace tugged Shola's big toe for a third time. Slowly, reluctantly, he returned from the land of dreams — where a dusky maiden had been giving him an all over body massage. He was displeased to find Grace, who bore no comparison to his dream masseuse, gripping his toe.

"Aah! Are you sick? I've been trying to wake you up. Mummy's calling you."

Shola smiled at his sister, then growled at her. She fled the room expecting to be chased. He got up and dragged his lanky frame into the living room still rubbing his eyes.

"Grace, go and play outside with your sister," Florence said softly when Shola appeared at the door.

"It's not fair. Why is it when adults want to talk we get sent outside?" Grace asked, folding her arms across her chest.

"Yeah. We always have to go outside and play," chimed Gloria, sitting next to her sister and adopting the same pose.

"You know, you are quite right," Florence said, after a moment's consideration.

The twins looked pleased with themselves.

"Why should you have to go outside and play all the time?" Florence continued. "Gloria you can go and wash the plates from this morning and Grace you go and take out the bin. After that you can iron your uniforms for tomorrow. Okay?"

"It's not fair," Grace said standing up.

"This is all your fault," Gloria accused her.

When they caught their mother's solemn stare, they retired to the kitchen grumbling under their breath.

Florence turned to Shola. "Close the door and sit down here."

He did as she asked. Already, he was beginning to dread the tone of his mother's voice.

"Shola, ever since we returned to this our country, I have been made to feel completely worthless."

Shola looked away from his mother's face.

"I've searched high and low for a job without success. Your father and I returned here because we thought that you and your sisters would be better off. I am glad you are taking your education seriously..."

"Mum, can I just ask, is this what you and Dad were quarrelling about last night?"

"You heard us?"

"I think the whole neighbourhood did. It was embarrassing."

Florence sighed. "Well, I am telling you now, so you know the full story. As I tried to explain to your father, Grandma 'Benin' is not very well. She can no longer look after her business, or herself for that matter. With your uncle in London and sister Jenny still in France, I am the only family nearby to take care of her. Since Lagos people will not give me a job, I will return to Benin, where I can stay in a rent free house and begin to feel like a person by running her business."

"Yeah, but..."

"But you children? Your father? Shola, at the rate we are going I could be in Lagos for five years and still be without a job. This is not just about looking after Mama, it is an opportunity for me. After all, I am not the one who dragged the family back to Nigeria, am I? If I am not achieving anything here, I might as well return to England. But I am sure this move to Benin will be a positive one."

"So you've decided."

"I have decided. Myself and the twins will leave next month, so I will have time to find them a school. You can come and visit us anytime you want."

"Is that it? I mean, how long will you stay in Benin?" Shola asked, trying to keep the conversation alive until the drug induced haze cleared from his mind.

"Only God knows."

"But surely..."

At that moment Isaiah stumbled into the living room carrying a crate of beer.

"So you are still wasting the little we have on drink?" Florence cried indignantly.

Shola shook his head. How his father had demeaned in stature. His mother wouldn't have dreamed of speaking to him like that in England. Their relationship had once been based on respect. But that was now a thing of the past.

"Don't talk about me, Mother of Shola. I say don't talk about me like that."

"Why not?"

"Talk about your son. Look at what he has been smoking."

Isaiah produced a stub in the palm of his hand. Florence looked disappointedly at Shola.

"So you smoke? I have suspected for some time now. But why? What do you gain from it? Don't you know that you're damaging your health? Haven't you read those government health warnings on the cigarette packet? Not to talk of how your breath will smell."

"If he smoked ordinary cigarettes that would be one thing," Isaiah interrupted. "But do you know what this is?"

"No... it is not," retorted Florence, shaking her head in disbelief.

"It is. Indian hemp. Smell it."

Isaiah pushed it under her nose, but Florence turned her head.

"Shola, why? Why this drug that turns people into mad men? Why?"

Shola sat, hanging his head. His mellow Sunday had been shattered. He stood up, unsure of where he was going. He just knew he had to get as far away from his parents as possible.

"Where are you going, can't you see we are talking to you?" Isaiah frowned.

"I need to get some air."

"Come here. Shola, we are still talking to you," his mother called in a more soothing voice.

"I'm sorry. I need to get out of here." Shola reached the front door, then stopped abruptly. "All I came home for was some peace and quiet. To study. That's all I came home for. But i can see that I'm not going to get any if I stay within these walls."

"Shola, come in and sit down, please. No one

is biting you."

Shola stared at his mother. "Mum, first you turn my world upside down by bringing me to Nigeria. But I coped, I adapted. Then you decide you are leaving Lagos for some outback town because no one will give you a job. D'you want to know the truth? Frankly, I'm pissed off with you."

"Aah! Shola-me!"

"And the last thing I need..." he turned his attention to his father, "the very last thing I need, is to be preached to about smoking grass by a drunkard."

Shola turned and stormed from the room.

"Drunkard! Who? You're calling me a drunkard?" Isaiah sprung from his armchair. "Shola, don't push me to curse you. Maybe you think this is insolence, it is more like madness. Hmmmn!"

Shola stood by the front door, shaking his head as his father ranted. "You abuse me, now you want to run away. If you step out of that door I will disown you."

Shola's heart hardened as his temper rose. A hatred he hadn't felt before consumed what little remained of the respect he once felt for his father.

"Disown me then. Who cares? Who wants to be owned by you anyway?"

"Sho-o-o-o-o-o-ola!"

Only the wind answered back through the open door.

* * *

Shola,
It has been four weeks since I told you of my dilemma and I still haven't heard from you. I know it's a lot to get your head around but that doesn't mean you couldn't drop me a line to show a little support.

Or is it because I mentioned that I was contemplating having a termination? You can't blame me for those thoughts every now and again. If it makes you feel any better, I am keeping the baby. But when I think of the lack of support from you and the thought of having to tell my parents, I almost wish that I had chosen a termination. It's not easy doing all this on your own, Shola. It really does take two.

That's right, Shola, I still haven't told my parents yet. I will soon start to show, I've already gained a few pounds and I can already feel movement, well it's more like a constant fluttering. All my jeans are already too tight for me and I've got a craving for peanut butter on chocolate digestives, might sound disgusting to you but it tastes absolutely divine to me.

Jokes aside, Shola — I think you should at least have the decency to write and be supportive while I'm going through all this. You don't know how much a few words from you mean to me at a time like this.

Shola, I have a surprise for you, I wasn't going to tell you but I've got a chance to come to Nigeria on a church exchange trip. I won't say anymore on the subject except that I'm determined to get a place on the trip.

I hope you can see from this letter that there won't be any hard feelings if you decide that I have to cope with the baby alone, but at least let me know soon.
With love, Jackie xxx

SUNSHINE AND RAIN

Shola saw the figure walking across campus towards him in the soaring heat and for one brief moment thought he was hallucinating. But as he continued towards her she stepped right into his path wearing a wide smile.

"Jackie?"

She beamed. "Surprise!"

"I don't believe it!" he cried as they hugged. "What are you doing in Nigeria, how comes you never told me you were coming?"

For the next few moments all they could do was grin and admire each other.

"Aren't you going to ask me why I came to Nigeria then?" Jackie asked eventually, realising that he could not have received her last letter.

"Er...yeah. I'm just so surprised." Shola was not only surprised and confused, there were several other emotions running wildly around his brain.

"I came to see you, of course. I missed you."

She moved closer and tickled the stubble under his chin. "I like this, it suits you... Oh, did you meet Josephine before you left London?" Jackie turned to introduce her companions. "She lives by your old manor."

"Hi, Shola, how are you," Josephine said.

"I'm cool. Nice to see you," Shola replied, noticing Jackie's friends for the first time.

"And this is Kate, Josephine's cousin. She's a student at this university too."

"Hi, I think I've seen you around," Shola said. "We've never been introduced though."

"I've seen you at parties," Kate confirmed as she and Shola shook hands.

"You're still organising parties then?" Jackie asked.

"You know me, Jackie. Anywhere there's good music, I'm never far behind."

"Are you people determined to roast today?" Kate asked, shielding her eyes from the sun. "Why don't we go and sit down in the shade?"

They strolled over to one of the shaded refreshment shacks located across the road from Moremi Hall.

Shola still couldn't believe she was in Nigeria. While he was waiting to pay for the sodas, he looked over at Jackie seated at the table. He considered how she had changed since he had last seen her. Adolescent fat was still noticeable on her face, but whereas it had once made her look cute and cuddly, now it softened her cheekbones giving her a look of sophisticated maturity. She had grown too. Her body was still in good proportions and her long legs were still the main feature. She wore her hair permed and swept back, giving her an air of elegance.

Shola couldn't understand how Jackie could be pregnant. He cast a glance at her stomach, five months down the road and she wasn't showing at all. He would have to wait until they had a moment together in private to bring up the subject, to apologise for not having written and told her how he felt about it. They had a lot to talk about, a lot of decisions to make. Moreover, now that she was here in Nigeria, Shola knew he had to create an opening for Jackie in his busy love life. He had only recently got back with Evelyn after a brief affair with a second year Mass Communications student. And now, she gave him less time to himself. "We can't have you succumbing to temptation, can we?" Evelyn justified, using his own excuse for his infidelity against him. She had almost perfected the practice of 'close marking' (a University of Lagos term used to describe people who were always seen on the arms of their partners). Shola's eyes darted around, half-expecting Evelyn to turn up at any minute.

Jackie caught his gaze and winked at him. As he took the drinks over to the table he wondered if she still felt the same way about him.

Shola placed the tray of drinks on the table. "So, how could you afford to get to Nigeria?" he asked.

"We're on a student exchange programme," Josephine answered. "See, every year the college students in our church group get to travel to a country in the Caribbean or Africa on this exchange programme and..."

"Steady on. Who asked you anyway?" Jackie quipped jokingly. Then, turning her attention to Shola, she continued. "As she said, each year we get to travel to Africa or the Caribbean, and the following year we get to invite the students we stayed with back to London."

"Yeah, this year we came to Nigeria because one of the sisters was looking for a lost love," Josephine teased.

Question answered, Shola thought.

"And what's wrong with that? Me and Shola go back a long way, you know," Jackie said, moving up close and hugging him. The other two girls exchanged knowing looks.

"So where are you guys staying?" Shola asked.

"They're staying at my house in Ikoyi," replied Kate proudly.

Shola nodded.

"And when are you going back to London?"

"On Sunday, unfortunately," Jackie added.

"What, the day after tomorrow?"

"I'm afraid so, lover boy. So you better get a move on," Josephine teased.

"But why didn't you come and see me earlier?"

"I've been looking for you every day for the last week. I've been bugging Kate to find out where I might find you."

"Problem was," Kate interceded, "all my friends know you as Selector."

"I never call myself anything but Shola. Selector comes from the sticker in front of my decks. Anyway, too late to put that right. But now that we've met up, we're gonna make the most of it. I don't know how you've found Nigeria up 'til now, but prepare to be entertained."

Shola suggested that he and Jackie take a long walk so that he could show her the sights. They took their leave of her companions who understood that Jackie and Shola had a lot of catching up to do.

"So, how do you feel about being a father?" Jackie asked him after he had apologised profusely for not having written very much.

"I don't really know," he replied. He caressed her small round stomach. "I've been so far away from it all, that I guess it hasn't really hit me. I don't think I can really feel like a father until the baby's here. But I am excited about it, a little anxious perhaps. I wouldn't have planned it this way, but now that it's happened I'm going to do my best to take responsibility for it."

"That's good to know," Jackie said. "But how do you intend on taking responsibility for the baby if you're in Nigeria and I'm in England?"

"Well, it will only be until I finish at university," said Shola. "It's just two and a half years to go, it will be over sooner than you think."

"Two and a half years," Jackie sighed, "by that time our baby will be preparing to go to university itself I imagine."

Shola laughed. "I wouldn't be surprised, the parents are both highly intelligent, so why not?"

In her heart, Jackie knew that Shola wasn't ready for fatherhood. He was right, he had been so far away from it unlike her, who lived with the reality of the baby every day. She didn't hold it against him, he was the same old Shola who had left London in the summer, while she wasn't the same Jackie, she couldn't possibly be. Yet she realised that she would wait for Shola as long as it took. He was her first real love and the father of her baby. As long as he wanted to be with her, she would want to be with him.

"Coffee, sugar, gin, grass, orange juice, lemon..."

"Never. No,no, no! Shola, come over here and hear what Abi's put in the punch."

Shola excused himself from Jackie and swaggered over to John and Abi on the other side of the room as music oozed out of the speakers.

"Repeat what you just told me," John requested.

"You want to know about making punch, yeah? Well, first you buy your bottles of gin and soak the coffee and gin for two days. That way people don't know they are getting drunk. Then you can add some sugar to take away the bitter taste of the coffee."

"Truly?" asked John, his eyes wide with anticipation.

"Believe!" confirmed Abi. "Then you add some weed..."

"You mean grass? 'Igbo'! As in, the one we smoke?" John broke into raucous laughter.

Abi and Shola grinned at each other. Then Shola took a gulp from his cup, savouring the taste.

"Is this really your first time of drinking Abi's punch?" Shola inquired.

John nodded.

"Where did you learn such a recipe, Abi?"

"From his father, Professor Uwe, the chemist."

The guys dissolved into fits of laughter.

"You wait 'til about ten o'clock, then watch the effect it's going to have... especially on the girls."

More raucous laughter emanated from their corner of the room. John surveyed the young, happy faces of the twenty or so people squashed into Abi and Shola's room on campus. There were two guys to every girl. His eyes settled on Kate. He had seen her around on campus, but had never had an excuse to get close to her. Tonight could be the night, he thought.

"Shola, when are you going to introduce me to your friends?" he implored.

"Whenever you're ready. Now?"

John hesitated.

"Alright," Shola said, taking another gulp of the punch. "In your own time." He turned back to his friends. "Hey, Abi, that's a stylish punch bowl," he said sarcastically, admiring the vessel decorated with silver foil and artificial leaves.

"Yeah, it's quite nice isn't it? Guess where I got it from?"

Shola shrugged.

"It's our bathing bucket."

The two burst out laughing. Just then, Jackie wandered over.

"What's so funny? A little thing among boys, or can anyone join in?"

"Have I been neglecting you?" Shola asked, feeling guilty.

"Well, you said it," she answered. "Come on, let's get some life into this party. The best thing at the moment is the punch. You know, Kate's already had four cups."

John beamed when he heard this and winked at Shola who gave him a sly grin.

"Okay. What's your pleasure... quick step or slow grind?" Shola asked, easing Jackie into the centre of the room to dance.

A lover's tune came on and Jackie immediately got in the groove. Shola, feeling in a particularly mellow mood, was not far behind. Soon, nearly everyone in the room was dancing cheek to cheek.

Except for John and Kate, who were embracing in a corner and Abi, who had taken a liking to Josephine. They were in another corner getting seriously acquainted. Abi's hands cupped Josephine's tight butt. Josephine, her arms around his neck, pulled him closer still.

Gradually, the punch got lower and the music got slower. Shola threw some more lover's music into the mix and the dancing continued slow and steady, nice and easy. Shola and Jackie danced close, relaxed in each other's arms.

Jackie was glad she had come to Nigeria. She had had some quality time with Shola and had managed to talk to him at great length about the baby on its way and their future together. Also, seeing Shola studying for a degree had filled her with determination to pursue her dream of studying Law. That was the way their relationship had been all along, they were always inspiring each other. But her life had taken so many turns in recent months that she didn't exactly know what she wanted to do anymore. The one thing she was sure of was that she still loved Shola. She could see that now.

Shola breathed lightly on Jackie's neck, kissing it softly. For some reason he felt sad. It seemed that no sooner had he and Jackie found each other, than they would be saying goodbye again.

All the time apart had not changed a thing between them. He still loved Jackie, and when he looked into her eyes was sure she felt the same. They had only spent a day together and already a future without her seemed inconceivable.

"It's hot in here, let's go for a walk," he told her, feeling an overwhelming need to be alone with her.

They slipped past the couples whispering words of love to one another in the corridor and out into the open air of an African night, a night as mixed as both their emotions. The breeze was persistent, but still the heat was stifling.

They walked out onto the main road that wound its way past the trees, with no particular destination in mind, both lost in their individual thoughts. They walked for what seemed to be miles, holding hands, secure in each other's company. Eventually they reached the lagoon front, where they listened to the sound of water lapping against the pebbled shore and watched the lights in the distance that illuminated the bridge leading to Lagos's exclusive Victoria Island neighbourhood.

Shola looked deep into Jackie's eyes, then kissed her gently. A lingering kiss. Jackie hugged him tightly, staring over his shoulder at the lagoon, wishing this night really would last forever. Then she kissed him, slowly, deeply, hungrily, until they were smothering each other and gasping for breath.

Their hands reached out, teasing, exploring and caressing each other. Shola steadied himself and stood back a little, searching Jackie's face for the answer he was looking for. They gazed at each other in silence, but it was obvious that what they both wanted more than anything else, was to spend the night together. Shola reached for her hand. He couldn't wait to get back to his room and get the party over with.

Jackie kept pace alongside him as they passed the mangrove swamp by the lagoon.

As they passed the shrubs that led away from the lagoon to the main library, Jackie pulled Shola after her, into the plantation and up against a nearby tree. She had longed for him for so many months and thought about their one night of passion so many times that she could barely wait for them to repeat the event.

The night sky offered very little light as they fumbled at each other's clothing. Shola never imagined Jackie to be like that, hardly able to contain herself. Shoving her hand down his boxers, she managed instant arousal but Shola didn't feel comfortable.

"Not here, Jackie," he managed to say.

Without a word, Jackie kissed him tenderly. Shola sighed, and his hands began to disobey him. He continued to undress her and eased her back against the tree. There, in the sultry warmth of an African night, they made love again.

On their way back to the University, Shola couldn't resist picking the locks of the campus swimming pool gates. He and Jackie undressed again and slipped into the pool. Jackie felt so relaxed, she wished she did not have to return to the hustle and bustle of London. She could easily see herself settling in a country like Nigeria, where everything seemed so laid back.

By the time they returned to the party, weary and fulfilled, the show was about over. Abi and Josephine were clearing up around the last two couples, still dancing to the low volume music.

"It's past midnight, Jackie. We'd better get

going," Josephine said.

Jackie looked around. "Where's Kate?"

Josephine shrugged. "I thought she was with you."

Shola and Abi looked at each other, exchanged winks and said, "John" in unison.

"Wow! She doesn't waste time," Jackie exclaimed.

"You can talk, madam," Josephine shot back.

But Kate wasn't in John's room. Jackie and Josephine then assumed that she had returned home to Ikoyi without them. In which case, instead of making their way back immediately, they decided to spend their last night in Nigeria thrashing Shola and Abi at Scrabble.

In the morning, Abi drove them to Ikoyi to pack and prepare for their journey home. It turned out that Kate had not returned home after all. Josephine decided that she must have spent the night at a friend's on campus instead of travelling home. Jackie was disappointed that she would not be able to say goodbye properly, since Kate had been such a splendid host. Once packed, she wrote her a note, then the foursome left for the airport. There were long moments of sad silence all the way there as Shola and Jackie sat impassively in the back seat, holding hands.

At the airport, Jackie and Josephine were greeted by the rest of their church group. As they went through the formalities of checking in, Shola looked out onto the runway not really noticing all the activity around him. He was beginning to feel choked up inside. If only Jackie didn't have to leave.

"Abi," he said suddenly, "tell the girls goodbye for me. I have to go."

"Go where?"

"I'll wait for you in the car. Just tell them for me."

"No." Abi shot back. "It's the last time you'll see her for a while. Tell her yourself."

Shola looked over to Jackie, who was backing away from her friends to come and join him. She approached smiling, but her smile was tinged with a sadness that matched his own.

She held both his hands in hers. "We have to go now," she said solemnly.

Shola nodded. His throat felt too tight to speak.

Jackie looked into his eyes. "Shola, will you promise me one thing?"

He nodded again.

"Say you'll promise."

His voice was just a whisper. "Promise."

"Keep in touch, okay? Reply to my letters."

Shola nodded.

Jackie hugged him and kissed him lightly on the lips, smiled and turned to leave.

"I'll keep you posted about the baby," she said blowing him a kiss.

Shola was still standing on that spot long after Jackie had disappeared from view. He took a moment to collect his thoughts before following Abi to the car.

WANTED

As soon as the car nosed into the drive, they knew something was wrong. Outside Professor Uwe's compound were two hurriedly parked vehicles, one a blue police estate car. Parked behind the Professor's Mercedes was a customised Mitsubishi van. Abi's father, still in his dressing gown, was talking to an officer on the balcony.

Abi headed into the compound fearing the worst. Shola followed behind in a daze.

The first thing they saw as they entered, was a body on the ground, covered by a blanket. Professor Uwe was shouting something at his son, slapping his head in rage. At this serious moment, the spliff that Abi and Shola had shared on the drive back from the airport was now taking effect. Everything seemed to be going in slow motion. As if in a trance, Shola cut through the commotion to where the body lay. Bending down, he reached out and pulled back the cover.

Then began the nightmare.

It was Kate.

She was so still, Shola needed no one to tell him she was dead.

It was some time before he was able to find out what had happened. Kate's body had been discovered by the gardener, behind the shed at the bottom of the garden. She had died after choking on her own vomit. The police had discovered that she was at Abi and Shola's party where she was served a drink laced with illegal drugs.

Shola, Abi and John had been at the campus security post half an hour when Professor Uwe turned up to sign their release forms. Neither Abi nor Shola had a word to say to each other. They were too shocked, too forlorn, to think of a coherent story that might exonerate them from blame.

Later that day, the three students were summoned individually for questioning at the local police station. Statements were taken from every person who had attended the party. Shola was shown a list of nine names and asked for any additional revellers. Jackie and Josephine were missing from the list. Shola knew there were many more present but he could not remember who and made no special effort to recall. Even at this crucial moment, grassing on his friends didn't sit too easily with him.

The police took his statement, in which he insisted he was not aware of the contents of the punch. He said all he could remember was that it tasted alcoholic.

When he returned to campus, Shola found that Professor Uwe had evicted him from his quarters. Abi was now to stay in the main house with his family. Shola was left with two options: find a place on campus to squat, or go home. He could not bear to be under the same roof as his father for longer than a few hours, so he opted to move in with John on campus.

The story spread across campus like wildfire, fuelled by sensationalist coverage in the national dailies. The most distorted headline Shola saw, screamed: 'Campus Girl Dies In Voodoo Ritual'. He stopped reading the papers after that particular article.

Throughout, Shola tried to keep a low profile. Whenever he did go out he saw fingers pointing and when he entered a room, conversations stopped. Even friends who he had thought were close, suddenly didn't know him. He realised that there wasn't much he could do about the whole situation but inside his emotions churned.

He attended the police station several times during that week while the investigations into the circumstances surrounding Kate's death were taking place. When, at the end of the week, it was confirmed that traces of cannabis had been found in the deceased's blood, the eager police chief felt he had no choice but to charge Shola and Abi with manslaughter. After all, the newspapers, spurred on by Kate's father who had flown over from England, were all calling for someone to pay for this attractive college girl's death. With the manslaughter charge, only Professor Uwe's influence prevented Shola and Abi being remanded that very day. But the price for Shola's freedom was the confiscation of his passport by the police, just in case he decided to flee the country

Once he had been identified as one of the ringleaders of the 'Indian Hemp' party, as it became known, Shola was expelled from university. He now had no choice but to return home, where Isaiah was in an angry preaching mode. Even Papa DaCosta had bitter words for his grandson and that hurt Shola more than anything his father could say. Shola knew right away that if he had to stay at home with his father, life was going to be one long stretch of guilt-trips and sermons. It was going to be hell.

After his brief trip home, Shola returned to the university and made his way to John's room ready to collect his belongings. As soon as he entered the room, he knew there was something wrong. It felt like he was stepping into a totally alien environment. This was nothing like the room he recently departed from.

A bespectacled student was lying on his bed. He looked up at Shola blankly, before marking the page of the book he was reading and rising from the bed.

"Where's John?" Shola enquired, half-knowing what the answer might be.

"You mean the person who had this room before?" the student asked removing his glasses.

"Yes, John. This is his room."

"Eh? Well, I was given this room today. As you can see I am still in the process of unpacking my..."

"What happened to all my things?"

"Don't ask me, ask security. They packed everything... cleared the room out."

"So they have my things now?"

"I think so."

Shola wandered down the corridor to find a student who could enlighten him on John's whereabouts. Man-o-war was the one that should be able to help, nothing moved on campus without his knowledge.

Shola made his way to his friend's room in the adjacent male hall. As soon as Shola opened the door, everyone fell silent. One by one, their eyes hurriedly averted his. After a few superficial greetings, Shola called Man-o-war outside to talk.

"What are you doing here, Shola?" Man-o-war asked in a harsh whisper.

Shola was unconcerned. "Yeah, yeah, yeah. Listen, do you know where John is?"

Man-o-war's expression changed. "John got suspended," he replied.

"Shit!"

Man-o-war looked around furtively as Shola digested the information.

"Listen, Shola, my friend... you are banned from being on campus, anyone seen in your company faces expulsion. I can't talk..."

Shola raised his hand. "I know, I understand."

"I must go."

Shola nodded. "Go safely. Yes?"

Man-o-war hurriedly shook his hand then headed back to his room.

"What about Abi?" Shola called out after him.

"Abi landed on his feet. He was given a transfer to the University of Ife."

As Shola turned to walk away, tears glazed his eyes. Why was life so unfair? Abi, the main culprit, the person who had laced the punch in the first place, was able to get a transfer to another university because his father had connections, while he was left in Lagos to face the music.

He paused at the exit to the hall. He considered going to the security post for his record decks — the only thing of value amongst his possessions. But he knew it would do no good. The guards would deny all knowledge of it. They had probably sold it to another student with DJing ambitions by now. He kept walking. He didn't know where he was going, neither did he care.

CHECK MATE

Dear Shola,
How are you? Missing us as much as we (yes, we) are missing you, I hope.

Shola, I am worried, Josephine rang me last night after she had attended church saying that the minister announced that one of the exchange students had died in a tragic accident involving some sort of foul play with drugs. Then she went on to say that when she got home she was informed that it was her cousin Kate, the girl that I stayed with on my trip. Do you know exactly what happened? I hope you, Abi and the crew are okay.

I've got to admit I was upset when you didn't reply to my last letter but now I've learned about this I'm worried. I know you're prone to getting in trouble, so let's hope you weren't connected in anyway.

Well, here's a report on Junior (that's what I've decided to call our child for the moment). My stomach is definitely growing, which is a good sign that your baby's healthy. My breasts are huge — I bet you wouldn't mind sucking them now! No, seriously Shola, I'm eating for two even though they say you shouldn't and my face is so round. My skin is glowing, my hair is at it's healthiest and my morning sickness is easing up.

Oh yes, I've told my parents now and, despite their initial anger, they've started accepting the fact and my mum is even talking to me again and Dad is acting civil towards me.

Oh, a bit of gossip; Josephine and I bumped into Colin while out shopping the other day. Well, it looks as if they hit it off straight away, they swapped numbers. I'll keep you up to date on that one.

Right, I'm off for now, see ya soon.
Love Jackie xxx

*   *   *

Koko bit off half a lobe from his kola nut and crunched it slowly. In the otherwise silent room, it sounded like footsteps on a pebbled beach. Koko was a nickname, which referred to the blackness of his skin being a similar hue to the black beans within the cocoa pod. Mallam stared at the card Koko had just played, a cigarette hanging limply from his lips. He placed his card on the table decisively, drew on the cigarette and flicked the ash on the floor.

Shola knew it was too late to quit. Much too late. There was too much at stake now.

Sheer desperation had led him to gamble the little money he had left. Professor Uwe, who had contacts everywhere and probably prior warning, had managed to get all charges dropped against his son. Shola was to face the manslaughter charge alone. He was angry and desperate, not having the contacts that had saved Abi and he had no reason to feel optimistic about the outcome of his trial. Even if he was not found guilty of manslaughter, with Nigeria's strict drugs law he was bound to be sent down with a long stretch for possession of cannabis. He had heard enough about Nigerian jails to know that they were an experience one should avoid by any means necessary. Now Shola had to win enough money to get a decent lawyer to defend him.

His mother had sent him as much money as she could, but it was not nearly enough. His father, meanwhile, said he had enough financial problems of his own and couldn't contribute to his legal costs. Shola had no other option but to gamble his mother's money in the hope of making up the shortfall. As his mother always said, 'There is more than one route to the marketplace'.

Mallam had no sympathy, he drummed his fingers on the table impatiently. Shola had his card halfway to the table, then he hesitated, he needed to be sure, he could not afford to lose. The air became thick with irritation. Frustrated by his own indecisiveness, Shola slapped the card on the table.

Man-o-war immediately grinned and reached for the untidy bundle of money in the middle. Koko held out his hand to stop him.

"Let's raise the stakes."

Man-o-war glanced at the remaining cards in his hand to reassure himself. "Okay," he shrugged.

Koko looked to Mallam, then Shola. Both nodded consent and more notes fluttered onto the sizeable pile of money.

Two observers who had lucked out of the game earlier, exchanged looks. One shook his head, the other took a deep breath.

It was all or nothing. Shola knew he was unlikely to make any gains tonight. His only thought now was to win back enough to return to the table the following night. Maybe his luck would be better then.

Koko flicked his card onto the table. Shola closed his eyes in disbelief. He was sure he had lost, it all depended on what Mallam played. He looked up just in time to catch an eye signal between Mallam and Koko. It was all he needed to confirm that they were in league.

Shola felt a fool. A rage began to rise within him. His mind replayed every instance when he'd been on a winning streak and Mallam or Koko had managed to snatch away his victory. He now knew why he was losing so badly. He thought of all the money he'd lost. He thought of his mother working her fingers to the bone to get it. Too much had been lost at this table.

He glanced over at Man-o-war, who met him with a steady gaze. From his expression, Shola knew that he too had realised the scam. He felt like getting physical, but he knew better. Even if he could overpower Mallam, he did not fancy his chances of taking on both him and Koko.

Mallam played his card. Then Shola played and Man-o-war followed. Koko scratched his chin and played again. Mallam took a long drag on his cigarette and stubbed it out on the table edge, then he tossed his last card onto the table nonchalantly. Man-o-war stared at Mallam's cards like some dreadful disease had been thrown onto the table.

It was Shola's turn to reveal. He looked at Man-o-war, whose puffy cheeks were twitching uncontrollably. He knew Man-o-war had lost his gamble. His mind raced to find a way out.

Just then, someone knocked on the door.

Mallam jerked his head up, a scowl on his face. "Play!" he commanded.

Shola glanced sideways, raising an eyebrow with disdain and held Mallam's stare.

"Just play the card," Mallam conceded, his voice less demanding.

Shola pointed to the door. Koko pointed to the money. Shola stared at the pile on the table. If only he was a magician, he thought, he could make the pile disappear into his pocket. He heard the person on the other side of the door identify himself. It was Koko's brother. He too was an occasional gambler.

At that exact moment, one of the regular local power cuts pitched the room into darkness.

Shola did not need a second invitation, he reached out for the pile and grabbed as many notes as possible, then leapt towards the door.

"What the... Stop him!" Koko screamed.

But Shola was too fast. He bolted out the door, knocking Koko's brother over in the process and ran blindly down the dark corridor clutching the money. Hurried footsteps and excited voices behind him gave chase. But by now, Shola knew that none of them stood a chance of catching him.

Shola did not stop running until he reached the lagoon front. He sat on the shore and counted the money he had snatched from the table. It was less than half of what he had started out with the night before. Pure desperation gripped him now. He looked across the lagoon, reminiscing about the few stolen moments he and Jackie had shared in that exact spot. Then he looked at the lights in the more affluent part of the city and wished that he, too, was part of that world.

All of a sudden, Shola remembered a man he had met at the market. He searched inside his wallet and found the card. It stated simply: *Alhaji Musa, General Trader.* At the time Shola had dismissed the Alhaji as a hustler, but now he was curious to find out if the man would be good to his word, of getting him to London at a fraction of the cost of a regular air ticket, and without a passport. When he got home that night, Shola gave the Alhaji a call and set up a meeting at a hotel in downtown Lagos.

The outside of the Bristol Hotel, located near the Tinubu Square was teeming with Alhajis and hustlers, buying and selling anything from jewellery to household items, and even currency.

It took a while for Shola to locate his man, but it took hardly any time at all for the Alhaji to state his business. He offered Shola a one-way ticket to London for a small fee to be held as a deposit. In return, Shola would body package balls of powder to an address in London. "It's just like eating mashed potato and shitting it out again," he laughed.

Shola began to sweat profusely. He might be innocent at this game, but he wasn't a fool. He had read about the so-called donkeys who agreed to swallow drugs as a way of smuggling them into countries. Sometimes the packages broke inside the stomach and unleashed the drugs directly into the bloodstream, causing a heart attack. Shola was desperate to get to England, but he hoped he would never be that desperate.

He levelled his eyes with the Alhaji's.

"No way!" he said.

The Alhaji shrugged resignedly.

Shola rose to leave, an expression of deep disappointment etched on his face. The Alhaji offered him his hand, but Shola ignored it. He had started to walk away when the Alhaji called him back.

"Come, sit down. I thought all you young men would do anything for money and women."

"Wrong turn. That's not me."

"Hmmm. But you are eager to travel, Bha?"

Shola remained silent.

"Okay, I know what I will do. I have a brother called Mohammed who works at Tin Can, would you like to travel by ship?"

Shola didn't have to answer, his eyes said it all. Now, this was a much more viable option.

STOWAWAY

Shola wondered whether it was physically possible to swim across the Atlantic. Perhaps no one had ever made an attempt before. If his present plan failed, he would consider being the first.

He had been trying to sleep. He sat on a squashed cardboard box, which cushioned him from the pitted concrete ground of the dockside, and stared ahead at the blank grey wall that kept preying eyes away from the goods arriving from overseas by boat. His back was rested against one of the concrete pillars that seemed to rise to the sky, mushrooming into a set of floodlights.

The foghorn sounded again, like the call of a lost elephant. As his date with destiny drew closer, Shola saw Mohammed flash a reassuring smile at him and responded with a thumbs up. He blanked out the details of what the immediate future held, preferring instead to concentrate on the bigger picture — his dream of getting back to

London to be with Jackie and, hopefully, in time for the birth of his baby. Now that he knew that he was not going to stay in Nigeria, Jackie emerged once again as the love of his life, the person he would most like to spend the rest of his days with.

He also dreamed of himself getting back behind the decks and spinning records again. He imagined himself a rising star in his chosen career, all around him the studio was a buzz as the broadcasters prepared to go on-air. Yet he was composed enough to give an eager young journalist a personal interview, on his meteoric rise from pirate DJ to drivetime host of the funkiest station in London. His producer signalled frantically for him to get rid of the journalist as his top-rated music/discussion programme was due on air within seconds. Then Shola turned confidently to the studio mike. *"Hello London! You came to get down, and have we got a party for you..."*

The foghorn heaved a final heavy sigh as the pilot boat gave way for the container vessel to cautiously approach its berth in the darkening gloom of Porto Novo. Mohammed knelt down in front of Shola, searching his face for any signs of nervousness.

"How do you feel? You feel good?"

Shola nodded.

"Alright! Soon, yeah?"

Shola nodded again, trying hard to remain calm. He shifted his attention to the thick mooring ropes being fed down from the vessel.

The floodlights were turned on, lighting the shuddering blue and white hull of the newly berthed ship to reveal the name of the vessel, *Hugh Boeier*, registered in Amsterdam. The shuddering ceased as the vessel's mighty engines ground to a halt.

Nearby, was a group of about fifty casual dockers, huddled in groups. The muslims among them were just concluding evening prayers, others were gambling. One or two gave him odd stares, but Shola avoided eye contact. It would have been easy for them to tell that he did not fit in with the other dock workers, for although a number of them also wore European attire, Shola's clothes were just a little too well cut, not over or undersized. Nor had the scars of hardship etched themselves on his features.

The Customs and Immigration officials appeared as the loading ramp was let down. Pleasantries were exchanged between them and the captain of the vessel as the Nigerian authorities concluded their official business. The captain disappeared to wherever a content looking captain disappears to having arrived safely at port, and the furious activity of loading and unloading a roll on-roll off container vessel began.

Shola felt his stomach rise. Mohammed smiled at him. Not long to go. Mohammed seemed to know everyone at dockside. He was even welcomed enthusiastically by the *Hugh Boeier's*

European crew.

Finally, Mohammed beckoned to him. The time had come.

"Stay close to me. It will be fine," he assured Shola.

Shola nodded and began to follow, certain that someone would stop him and demand to know what business he had on board the ship.

He banished any negative thoughts from his mind and assumed the role of a casual worker under Mohammed's command. He loosened some buttons on his shirt and turned up the collar, then stepped out of his leather slip-ons and trampled on the heels, wearing them as flip-flops in order to blend in with the other dock workers. Getting even more into character, he began to walk like a man who had spent his entire life loading and unloading heavy goods.

Mohammed kept walking. Shola kept pace with him, past the three European crew members supervising the unloading of brand new European vehicles. Mohammed looked around furtively before disappearing through a door and Shola followed quickly behind. No one seemed to notice them. They descended two flights of steps before emerging onto a dimly-lit cargo deck. They wandered between the rows of containers until they found a suitably concealed spot.

"It's okay here," Mohammed said.

Shola nodded.

Mohammed grasped his hand with both of his. "Allah be with you."

"Thanks."

Mohammed turned to leave.

A sensation of freedom travelled the length of Shola's body. Soon he would be leaving behind his failure, starting a new life. A life of independence, where he would realise his dreams of establishing a career in the music business. He could see it now — SOLA RECORDS — Sounds Of Lasting Appreciation — or something along those lines.

Mohammed had told him to allow sufficient time for the ship to clear Nigerian waters. This gave him the next few hours for rest to rejuvenate himself in view of the challenge ahead.

THE CRIME OF THE POOR

Daybreak. Shola glanced at his watch when he awoke. He had been in his hiding place for ten hours. The ship's lurching movements and the noise of the engine indicated that it was now on its journey. He was hungry and thirsty. He had forgotten how long a human being could last without water, but remembered it was not very long. He decided to go in search of the crew to inform them of his presence on board. That way he would at least get to eat and drink.

He moved cautiously between the containers and out onto the main deck. The clear blue water of the ocean greeted him. He took a deep long breath of sea air and felt revived. He wandered around the deck and peered into a porthole, through which he saw three men playing cards. One of the men stood up slowly and stared directly at him as if he were an alien. The other two followed his gaze. Without breaking eye contact the man came out onto the deck towards him.

"Speak English? Parlez Francais?" the man enquired.

"English," Shola answered.

"You come on board in Nigeria?"

"Yes. Nigeria."

"How many?"

"How many what?"

"How many more?"

"How many more what?"

"Ahhh! You are playing games, eh? Come with me."

Shola followed him to an adjacent cabin. The man stepped aside to let him pass and Shola entered. The man then bolted him in from outside.

Shola didn't have to wait long. He heard voices outside, then the door opened. A short man with a moustache walked menacingly towards him. Shola backed away slowly as the man circled him, like a hyena waiting for an opportune moment to strike. When he did, it was with a quick fist to Shola's stomach leaving him too stunned to respond.

The man threw a few more blows.

"Where are your friends?" he demanded.

"Who?"

"The ones who came on board with you. Where are they hiding?"

"I came alone. Just me," Shola replied defiantly.

"Don't try to fool me. I know all your tricks.

You people always stowaway in groups."

"I'm here alone."

"Are you sure?"

Shola nodded. The man peered into his eyes to check for sincerity before interrogating him further. "You have a passport?"

Shola shook his head. The man eyed him suspiciously.

"So you are Nigerian."

"No."

"But you live in Nigeria?"

"No. I live in London."

"London? But you have friends, relatives you stay with in Nigeria?"

"Yes."

"In Lagos?"

"Yes. In Lagos."

"So you are Nigerian from Lagos."

"No. I'm British. I'm from London."

"And you say you are the only one on board?"

"Yes. The only one. Just me."

The man studied him closely.

"Wait here." The man departed, bolting the cabin door behind him.

Shola was glad to see him go. He clutched at his stomach, only now did he allow himself to feel any pain. He sat down, glad for a chance to gather his thoughts, wondering what the crew's next line of action would be. He closed his eyes and said a short prayer, asking for deliverance.

He looked up at the sound of the door unbolting. The man with the moustache appeared again.

"Follow me," he told Shola.

Shola trailed behind him onto the main deck where the man spoke to one of the crew in German. Then the man turned to him and said, "This man will give you work. Don't give him trouble or else I will lock you up..."

By nightfall Shola was shattered, having finished the hardest working day of his life. He had been instructed to do what he thought was a simple job of scrubbing the deck. Finally, after twelve hours of solid work and with no light with which to work further, he was allowed to rest. He was totally exhausted and needed to rest his back. Blisters had formed on both his hands. Shola asked for ointment to apply to his wounds, but the crew just laughed and shut him away inside an empty cargo container.

He awoke when the container was opened and bright sunlight streamed in. The ship had docked at an African port and the man with the moustache appeared. He marched Shola quickly down the ship's gangway.

"What country is this?" Shola asked, looking around him. From the look of things he was still in Africa.

"Mr Lagos, you are now in Gabon," the man with the moustache replied with a sneer.

Shola's worst fears were confirmed. His scant geography told him that the ship had sailed south along the African coast, away from England.

"You will stay off my ship, do you understand?" the man said threateningly.

"You can't just leave me here," Shola insisted.

"I can and I will. Or would you like me to call the port authorities and have you arrested? I've warned you, stay off my ship. Next time, I will not be so kind."

With that the man climbed back up to the main deck of his ship and stood watch.

How could one person bear so much bad luck, Shola wondered. He was actually further away from his destination than when he started out in Nigeria, and now he had to start all over again and find another ship to stowaway on. He wondered why his mother was so fond of saying, "No matter how bad things turn out, there's always a reason to be thankful to God." Right at this moment, Shola could not think of one. He turned his back and headed away from the port.

> Dear Jackie,
> When you receive this letter you will probably already know the full story of what happened when you departed the campus. Things got really bad for me in Nigeria and kept getting worse. Myself and Abi were both expelled from university because of the scandal.
>
> The authorities confiscated my passport and advised me to seek a

good lawyer. Unfortunately, I do not have sufficient funds to cover that, Mum gave me what she could but it wasn't enough. Dad refuses to help me. He says it's about time I faced up to my responsibilities.

What I am about to tell you may sound a little drastic but I assure you it is the only way out of this no-win situation. I have decided to stowaway. It's the only way I can get back to London without my passport. I know it sounds dangerous but, trust me, I will be back in your loving arms sooner than you think. My first attempt failed but, if at first you don't succeed...

Jackie, I can't wait to feel your body next to mine, as I write these words I feel my nature rising. I can almost taste you as I recall the few passionate moments that we have shared. The things I'm going to do to you is nobody's business, that's if you allow me. I've been such a pig lately, I should have written before now but I hope you'll understand. Don't worry, I intend to make it up to you best I can.

Be with you soon
Shola xxx

*   *   *

Libreville, Gabon, Shola mused as he was walking along the tree lined streets of the capital city. The streets were devoid of traders or hawkers, unlike Lagos. And it had a cleaner, less hurried, atmosphere. There were less irate beeping of car horns, revving engines and fewer pedestrians cursing motorists. The most apparent difference in the traffic was the number of functional traffic lights in the city and the fact that the drivers actually seemed to obey the signals. In Lagos, it was a case of first come, first serve.

It was frustrating trying to decipher what was being said in the local mixture of French and patois, but somehow Shola's GCSE French came flooding back to him in his hour of need. Slowly at first, but then after a while he surprised himself with his fluency.

"Anglais?"

"Yes."

"Lagos boy, enh? Smoke?" The man offered Shola a cigarette.

Shola hesitated. He wasn't in the habit of accepting gifts from strange men who came up to him in a bar.

"Don't insult me. You know it is an insult to enter the king's house and not join the feast."

Shola accepted the cigarette.

"So, Lagos boy, why are you here?" the man asked.

"I'm not too sure."

"Hmm. Me too. I'm not sure why I'm here getting drunk. Nobody is sure. But why do you think you're here?"

Shola drew deeply on his cigarette. He really didn't know why he had wandered into the bar to use up one of the few U.S. dollars he had in his possession. He just felt that a glass of beer would cheer him up.

"I was on board a ship illegally, trying to make my way to England. The ship landed in Gabon and they threw me off."

"Ahh! So you are stealing ship."

"No. I didn't steal nothing."

"You Lagos boys love to steal ships too much."

"You mean stowaway?"

"I know many people who steal ships. One very good friend, he never return since." The man blew cigarette smoke slowly towards the ceiling. "But anyway…"

"Why are you here?" Shola ventured to ask.

"Me? For sleeping with another man's wife," the man laughed.

"What's so funny?"

"I've been in jail because of it and who do you think was responsible for that?"

"The man's wife?"

"Who else!" He chuckled like a train gathering speed.

Shola joined in the laughter.

"They kept me in detention for six months."

"Six months!"

"But they can't take me to court because they have no case. That is how we poor men suffer. At least now I can live like a king again." He raised his glass of beer and let out an ironic laugh.

The man introduced himself as Dupair. As they chatted, Shola discovered that Dupair had lived an extremely exciting life. He had been a sailor and lived in Lagos for three years, travelled in Europe, through Belgium and France, and within Africa, to Cameroon, Nairobi and Kenya. Dupair explained that nowadays ships crews were liable for every stowaway on board. That was why Shola was unceremoniously dumped in Gabon. They didn't want any responsibility for him.

Dupair explained that he made a living by scrounging work from docked ships and undertaking casual work at the docks, while dreaming of one day returning to his life as a sailor. He would surely be able to help Shola.

"I need to lie low for a while," Shola said, "Do you think I can stay at your place?"

Dupair laughed. "Lie low? Do you know where I sleep?"

"Wherever you sleep is good enough for me."

"Why not. If you want to see how we people live. Why not! You are welcome."

Shola was surprised at the number of bottles Dupair consumed without appearing to be any worse than when he started. Long after Shola had switched to Shandy, Dupair kept dancing and drinking, until two in the morning when the homeless and those too drunk to move were pushed out of the bar.

The shanty town on the outskirts of Libreville that Dupair lived in, was full of unauthorised buildings based around an infrequently used railway track. Most of the shops in the area doubled as bedrooms at night and were constructed above the mosquito infested swampland around the railway line and built from old wooden planks, cardboard and corrugated iron sheets.

The flimsy shacks had mushroomed into a small independent district, with its own bars, hairdressers, canteens and betting shops. The district's inhabitants were made up mainly of immigrants from other West African states.

Dupair stopped by a set of wooden doors and steadied himself to open the padlock. Even when open, it was a squeeze to get through. One big step took Shola to the centre of the room.

Dupair's place was basic to say the least. It didn't take him long to spread out a mat and fall asleep.

Shola was as near as he had got all night to falling asleep when a scratching sound brought him to full consciousness. He sat up abruptly, to discover, horror of horrors, rats scampering about. Even after chasing them out of sight, Shola couldn't get another wink of sleep that night.

The next morning, Dupair treated Shola to a filling breakfast at a local stall. Then they made their way to the docks to look for work. As they went, Shola told Dupair of his first stowaway adventure. Dupair listened intently, then advised Shola to find a partner if he intended to stowaway again. He explained that in his opinion, as a former sailor, it was safer to stowaway in pairs.

Shola spent the day tracking Dupair from ship to ship enquiring about work, securing some half promises to return the next day for loading.

Back in the shanty town that evening, they went out to buy supper. Dupair introduced Shola to a rice dish cooked Ghanaian style, with ginger root, fried pepper and sautéed onions forming the glistening red sauce that slithered down the sides of the mountain of rice on his plate.

They sat beside the railway line, eating the delicacy under the light of a kerosene lamp and calling out to their acquaintances who passed by. In both directions and along both sides of the tracks, roadside traders had laid out their wares, the flickering lights from their lamps stretching far into the distance.

By the time they returned to Dupair's place, the rats were already partying on the roof. The two friends conversed late into the night, before drifting off to sleep.

The rest of the week followed the same pattern. Wake up early, down to the docks where sometimes they would get work but more often than not they wouldn't, back to the shanty town and the rat-infested shack to sleep.

One afternoon, Shola took a stroll by the

waterfront to see if he could find a ship heading for London. He hadn't gone very far when he stumbled upon an angry crowd chasing a teenager with a small box under his arm. Suddenly, from round a corner, a police vehicle appeared, also giving chase. The sight of the police car seemed to frighten the youth more than the mob which pursued him. He headed straight for the waterfront and without hesitation dived into the muddy waters below.

The crowd reached the dockside and stood peering down, but there was no sign of the youth in the swirling mass of brown water.

"Somebody help him!" Shola cried out in English despite himself.

An eccentrically dressed man beside him, turned and spoke in perfect English.

"Why do you want to help him? Do you know the boy?" he asked.

Shola shook his head. "No, but..."

"Then don't worry about it. It is not your business. And anyway, the boy is alright, he has simply swum to the sewage outlet further along the waterfront. That is the escape route most of these boys use. Believe me, I see this nearly every day. You know, they would have killed that boy, when all he needs is a thorough thrashing."

"Every day?"

"Mmm. Sometimes they are caught and flogged, sometimes they escape. I once saw a boy, no older than fourteen of fifteen, get stoned to death just for petty stealing."

"You know he got away with that box."

"Good luck to him. He has certainly earned it after his magnificent escape."

"Do you work in the docks?"

The man laughed, a laugh as warm as the day.

"Are you a journalist?" he asked Shola between chuckles.

Shola caught himself, refraining from asking the thousand and one questions on his mind.

"I'm going to get a coke," the man informed him. "You can join me if you want to."

They strolled towards a stall in the shade.

"You are from England... southern England. Probably London. Am I right?"

"How do you know?" Shola asked impressed by the man's precision.

"Why wouldn't I? You have also lived in Nigeria. It's in your accent?"

"Right again! Ok, tell me what I'm doing here?"

"You? You are here to stowaway."

Shola stopped in his stride. Was his desire to stowaway so great that he could be read like an open book?

The man smiled. "Come on. That was a lucky guess, but I know a few things. Why do you think they call me the Captain."

They reached the shade of the stall and one of its patrons hailed the Captain as he approached.

"Kapo!"

"Captain."

"I salute you, Sir."

He received his praise gratefully then sat in the shade, with Shola, sipping on his coke.

Shola finished his lemonade in large gulps and took time to study the Captain. He wore a white sailor's cap with an anchor insignia on the peak, a navy blue cotton shirt open at the top, with a blue and yellow scarf round his collar. His grey trousers were folded into his white socks and contrasted with his shiny black plastic shoes. He was in his mid thirties and explained that he was from Ghana, but had been stuck in Gabon for the last twelve months on 'business', without specifying what that business was. The Captain reminded Shola of a scoutmaster.

Shola and Kapo — as he preferred to be called — spent the rest of the day becoming acquainted, as Shola re-lived his stowaway experiences and Kapo, in turn, told of his life on the move.

Kapo had never known his father but travelled all of Ghana with his mother, who worked for a theatre group. When the work dried up, she was forced into prostitution to feed her family. At the time Kapo had thought himself lucky to have had so many 'uncles' who came to frequent his mother's shebeen. Never did the villagers of any community allow his mother to run her thinly-disguised brothels for too long however. Whenever she was exposed it was time to take to the road again.

"How many of you were there?" Shola asked.

"Five. All boys. None from the same father," Kapo stated matter-of-factly. "As the eldest, I was expected to help support the family. For a long time, I was a jack-of-all-trades to make ends meet. At fourteen, I decided to try my luck in Accra. To see if I could make it in the big city. My first job was as a messenger for the ministry. As you can imagine, the wages were bad... Oh! My salary was so miserable, I had to sleep rough to be able to send my mother money at the end of the month." Kapo became lost in his own thoughts for a moment, before proceeding with his story. "That's when I first visited the docks, started work as a casual labourer. I was young and wanted to see the world and that's when I started stowing away on ships. I have stowed away on more vessels than I care to remember, usually in search of a better standard of living, but sometimes just for the sake of adventure."

Kapo neither drank alcohol nor smoked. Never had, never would. He appeared to Shola to be a ladies' man, but when Shola brought up the topic Kapo told him he could not remember the last time he had been with a woman. He admitted a yearning for female company, but said he would not go out of his way to get it.

"My only vice," Kapo informed him, "is gambling. I am an addict."

As they later walked along the waterfront, Kapo informed Shola of all the exciting things he could do in Libreville.

"You sound like a tourist guide," Shola told him.

"That is good," Kapo laughed. "Because that's

how I earn my living. I take sailors around the city, showing them where they can drink and mingle with the ladies of the night."

They stopped on the quayside as a container vessel was coming into berth. The dockers were already securing the mooring ropes. With the vessel secured and the gangway in position, a small crowd gathered to go on board.

Soon the immigration officials appeared on the gangway. The jostling increased between dock officials, clearing agents and others concerned with the ship's business. Kapo pushed his way to the front and a uniformed guard let him through as soon as a crew member declared the gangway open. But the guard blocked Shola's path.

Kapo, who was halfway up the gangway, retraced his steps to confront the guard as others climbed the steps up to the deck.

"Please, let him through, my friend," Kapo said in French.

"Why? Who is he?"

For the first time Shola saw Kapo's expression become stony. He stared at the guard and jerked his head indicating that Shola be let through. The guard, caught in two minds, opted for a confrontation.

"Why?" he asked again. "I have given you a chance. Why him?"

"Have you ever asked me for any of the gifts I have ever given you?" Kapo asked earnestly.

The guard fell silent, unable to find a suitable reply. He stood aside and let Shola through.

"Thank you," Kapo responded. His familiar expression returning as he climbed on board.

On the deck, they were met by a Filipino crew member. Kapo greeted him in a few choice words of Filipino, which brought a smile of appreciation as they shook hands enthusiastically.

There was so much activity on the deck. Shola followed Kapo to the crew's quarters where Kapo and another crew member squared up for some wrestling horseplay. The other crew members cheered as Kapo eventually gave in a little too easily to a three count submission via an armlock. Already he had laid the foundation for a continued working relationship.

The crew revealed that they would be in port for four days. After much deliberation over the establishments they had visited the last time they docked in Libreville, the crew finally agreed to go along with Kapo's recommendation of a new hotel in town.

Kapo met them later with transportation. He had chartered a Volkswagen van for the evening. The crew climbed on board, looking quite different in their smart Hawaiian shirts and khaki shorts.

Throughout the ten minute drive, Kapo kept everyone in stitches with his jokes as the driver raced along, swerving round corners like he had a death wish. They arrived sooner than expected at the hotel.

Shola thought the hotel decor, a confluence of Western, Eastern and African design, was overdone to the point of being tacky. Then again, he reasoned, the clientele were not here to study the furnishings. Not unless they had breasts and were game for sex. There were girls galore.

Drinks were ordered and the group settled in the casino.

After a single round at the card table Shola became bored. Besides, gambling held too many bitter memories for him. He left the group and wandered through the casino onto the terrace overlooking the ocean. He absorbed the serene setting for a while, before returning inside to check out the hotel disco. The DJ was warming the house with some highlife music. There was no one on the dancefloor. A few couples and a foursome hugged the dark cubicles that surrounded the parquet dancefloor. So Shola returned to the casino, where Kapo was winning. One of the crew had already dropped out of the game, having lost all his money. Kapo had also lost a few games, but won about four for every game he lost.

Kapo spent the whole night in the casino. At one time, it seemed to Shola, he had won enough money for a flight ticket back to Ghana.

The next two nights saw Kapo and Shola take a different set of crew members out on the town. Kapo was again triumphant at the card table.

Kapo and Shola were at the dockside on the fourth day when the Filipino sailors all returned to their ship and sailed for Liberia. Kapo took off his cap and waved like a little boy, clutching the expensive watch that an officer had given him in appreciation of the wild night he had enjoyed on his first trip to Gabon. Kapo sold the watch and with the money and his gambling winnings he went to purchase an updated version of his uniform. He also bought Shola a new pair of blue jeans to replace the now tatty ones he wore.

In such good spirits, Kapo promised to get Shola on board a ship that would sail direct to Europe, but that might take a little time. Meanwhile, they would spend the next three days having one long party with the rest of the money, Kapo insisted.

For the next week Kapo was unable to secure any more lucrative escort jobs. Only two ships had come into the main port and he was beaten on both counts by other hustlers volunteering their services to the crew members.

Then their fortune changed. Kapo secured a deal smuggling six ladies of easy virtue onto a ship registered in Limassol. He was paid handsomely for the arrangement and, once again, he and Shola partied for the next two nights as if there was no tomorrow to worry about.

Then Kapo informed Shola that he had met a contact and had already made plans for him to stowaway on board a container ship destined for Europe, later in the week.

ABOARD AGAIN

Kapo stood inside the empty container shaking his head, still surprised that he had allowed Shola to talk him into accompanying him on his voyage. The last time he had stowed away he had vowed never to repeat the experience, having reached a stage in life where time and age had dulled his taste for excitement and adventure.

Kapo had learned, through one of his associates that the ship was destined for a French port. They had no time to waste.

Shola had said a hurried goodbye to Dupair and thanked him for his hospitality. Dupair had made him promise to send him a letter when he arrived in London.

Shola bought cigarettes and mineral water to last until they would have to declare themselves to the crew. Kapo then got the clearing agent to turn the other way, while his contact secured them within one of the very last containers to be loaded on board the Panamanian registered

Azuero Reefer.

Except for rays of light streaming through its air vents, the container was dark, but Shola's eyes soon adjusted and, before long the two stowaways were able to make each other out.

Kapo's contact had attached a thin piece of wire onto the latch before fastening the container's doors, to enable the stowaways to open the latch from inside, but otherwise it was identical to the scores of other containers on board.

Once they were settled, Shola turned to his companion.

"Kapo. I want you to promise me something..."

"What is that?"

"Place your hand on your heart and promise me, that no matter what, we will not leave this container until at least eight days have passed."

Kapo laughed. "I can do better than that. Come here."

Shola moved forward and Kapo took both his hands, as they sat cross-legged facing each other. He intertwined their fingers and placed their palms flat on the floor of the container.

"Akan, you are our witness. Yemanja, you are our witness. May you bring misfortune to the home of the person who suggests that we leave this place without good reason before eight days have passed. Not only to his home, but to the home of his parents, his brothers and to his children yet unborn." Kapo released Shola's fingers. "Is that good enough for you?"

"Bwoy! No need to get so deep, y'know," Shola smiled. "I was just trying to make sure that we were of the same mind."

Less than an hour later they could feel the container swaying in the air before coming to rest on deck with a bump. Shortly after, the ship left port.

Roget lay on the bunk in his cabin, staring at the ceiling and scratching his beard as he pondered his future.

This was his eighth year of sailing with the *Azuero Reefer*. It was twenty-four years since he first stepped aboard a ship as a crew member.

His father had been a Chef d'Escadre in the French navy, before retiring to the south of France with a small sailing vessel he had bought for leisure and pleasure. Roget first went to sea at the age of five and by the time he was seven, he knew he wanted a life at sea. But two years at the naval training base in Toulon soon extinguished his desire to follow in his father's footsteps.

After his dismissal from the navy for threatening to dismember a senior officer who had wronged him, Roget had embarked on a period of travel through French Africa before joining the merchant shipping trade. Because of his academic failure and the lack of a mentor in the world of merchant shipping, his progress had been slow. He was regarded as being without ambition. He knew different. He wanted to go all the way to the top.

The captain of the *Azuero Reefer* was due to retire at the end of this year. It would be a golden opportunity for the deputy to take over. Nobody knew the *Azuero Reefer* better than he did. The shipping company would have no choice but to appoint him.

He had been chief officer on the ship for five years now, five years too long and he felt that he should have been made captain before Wall, the Englishman brought in to command the *Azuero Reefer*. This time he would leave no stone unturned to get that job, and would make the shipping company aware that he could profit them by thousands, maybe even millions of pounds every year.

Roget swung his legs to the floor, opened his cabin door and wandered outside onto the deck, thinking of all the changes he would implement as soon as he took command of the ship. He leaned against the rail looking to the aft as the ship glided through the dark sea.

He could make out a row of lights on the horizon. By his reckoning they were passing the coast of Guinea. They had left Sierra Leone earlier and were travelling north-west to round the bulge of Africa. He was glad that Sierra Leone was the last port of call in Africa. He was looking forward to the week of plain sailing before the next stop in Europe.

He strolled towards the door nearest his cabin

and tried to push the handle down, but there was resistance. He looked up through the glass. Standing on the other side of the door with a plate of food in his hand, was an African. Roget, startled, jumped back. Both men were as surprised as each other, but Roget recovered first. He gripped the handle with both hands and tried to force the door open, but as hard as he tried, the stowaway held fast. He was even smiling at Roget.

Roget grew angry, growling and cursing. Eventually, the African released the door handle in a vain attempt to escape. Roget rushed in and seized him by the collar, pinning him against the wall. He felt like pulverising him and when the African winked and offered him a sandwich from the plate he still held, it was the last straw.

"You cheeky little..." Roget butted him in the face, bloodying his nose. When he saw the African's shocked expression, the chief officer grinned. "Ah, you understand. That's much better."

Roget attempted to drag his prisoner along the deck by his shirt which ripped as the African stood his ground.

"My shirt! My shirt! Look what you have done to my shirt!" he protested indignantly.

Roget felt his blood charging. He had dealt with several stowaways in his time, but none as cocky as this. He had only been challenged to a fight by a stowaway once and that time it had lasted a full ten minutes. On that occasion, he had triumphed in front of the cheering crew members, but he didn't fancy his chances of fighting this big one alone, on this deserted deck.

He decided guile was his best tactic until he could get others to support him. Roget reached for a sandwich, munched on it, and nodded to the African. The African nodded back.

Roget took the plate from him and motioned for the man to follow him. He led him to the crew's galley and offered him a cold beer.

The African eyed the bottle. "I don't drink beer." he said.

Roget shrugged, then opened the fridge door and invited the African to make his choice. Roget left him struggling to choose from the well-stocked fridge. The African called out after him, "Go and tell the captain I am here. I will eat and drink my bellyfull before you return."

He only had time to down half a can of cola by the time Roget returned with a dog, a truncheon and a blond mountain of a man. The demeanour of the chief officer was now hostile. Roget was cursing and swearing, the pupils of his eyes dilating, as he fixed the African a mean stare.

With the truncheon, Roget knocked the can of cola out of the stowaway's hand and sent it flying. The African kept a close eye on the growling dog. Roget barked an instruction at his huge blond companion, who stepped forward, clasped the African tightly by the wrist and led him out onto the deck.

* * *

Captain Wall stood in front of the African, unblinking. He waited for the captive to show some respect, or even a hint of fear. But he waited in vain. The African simply eyeballed him.

"What the hell are you doing on my ship?" Wall shouted in the African's face. He didn't wait for an answer. "I ought to let them string you from the rafters and lash you 'til you beg for mercy. You smug sonofabitch."

He then withdrew in a huff, telling Roget to "sort him out".

That was the type of order Roget relished. It was just like the captain to leave his chief officer to do his dirty work for him. Roget poked his prisoner in the shoulder with the truncheon.

"You heard what the captain said. I'm going to teach you a lesson."

The African shot him a dark stare, Roget's eyes lit up. That was just the response he was looking for. He wanted the African to put up a fight. How dare he come aboard the *Azuero Reefer*. He was going to humble and educate this backward stowaway.

He told Blondie, the burly sailor, to let the prisoner go then, with all his force, he lunged forward and whacked the African in the ribs with the truncheon, leaving the stowaway doubled over in pain. Then Roget hit him again and again. The final blow to the side of the head knocked the stowaway backwards with such force that he fell, his head hitting the deck with a sickening thud.

Roget allowed himself a satisfied smirk at the sight of the lifeless body. He called for the captain, who joined him soon after.

"He fell," Roget said convincingly, pointing at the body sprawled out on the ground in front of him.

"Well, okay, but are we going to stand here and have an inquest, or are you going to get rid of the body? Throw him overboard," the captain ordered. "And clean up this mess."

Roget nodded and, together with Blondie, scooped up the remains of the stowaway and tipped him into the sea.

A mournful shriek that pierced the night air sent a shiver through the three men. They looked at each other, fear in their eyes.

"There must be more of them," Wall said.

"What do we do now?" Blondie asked.

"We find them and..." Roget ran his finger across his throat, "give them what they deserves."

SEARCHING

Dear Shola,
I don't know why I'm writing these few lines but I am. I doubt you even read my letters anymore. I don't know what it is, I must be stupid, but something tells me to hang on, not to give up on you.

Right now I look more like a beached whale than a woman with child, I'm sure. Shola, the midwife asked me who will be present at the birth with me. Well, you can imagine that really depressed me as I don't have anyone who I think should be there except you. My mum won't come, as she said the other day, "You made your bed, you lie in it."

They threatened to keep me in the

hospital the other day because they found blood in my urine but after running some extensive tests they said I could go home as long as I put my feet up. I'm swelling everywhere even in places that I shouldn't be yet; ankles, fingers etc. They say I have to go for weekly check-ups instead of monthly. They say everything will be alright as long as I get plenty of rest.

Enough of my complaining, let me fill you in on the local gossip. Colin and Josephine are an item now, they've been seeing each other for at least a month, Josephine swears blind it's love. Patrick and his girl are back together, he's not messing around this time — I heard he's asked her to marry him. Richard has left college to pursue his career as a shop manager, yes he got promoted and he seems to think this is what he wants, I think he's crazy throwing away all that education to work behind a shop counter but each to his own.

Take care of yourself until you find the time to put pen to paper or until you hear from me again. Although you're neglecting me and your responsibilities, I still love you,
Jackie xxx

*   *   *

Shola downed the last drops from the water bottle. Their meagre supplies were dwindling fast. They were down to a bottle of water and a pack of Marlboro. They had been shut in the container for several days on a diet of sugar, water and cigarettes. Shola was growing weary of the darkness. Even with Kapo at his side for company, he craved to see a clear blue sky or moonlit night.

Kapo had been a pillar of strength to Shola. He was a man of so many stories. Earlier in the day when Shola had felt low, Kapo had told him the story of how six years ago, on his second stowaway trip, he had lasted for twelve days without food. He and his friend had survived the trip to Istanbul without leaving their hiding place and then managed to sneak off the ship without being detected.

On that occasion Kapo's luck ran out when he had hitched a ride not far from the port. The first vehicle that stopped for him was a police van. His friend had realised the danger first and had disappeared quickly, leaving Kapo to stand alone in the glare of the van's headlights. During the lengthy interrogation that followed, Kapo held fast, refusing to give details of the ship he boarded to Istanbul. Nevertheless, he was deported two weeks later.

"What about your friend?" Shola asked.

"I've never heard from him since. A success

story? Who knows? I like to think so. Maybe he's enjoying life in Europe, even as we speak."

Shola liked that idea and Kapo's story renewed his resolve.

"Tell me more about this your girlfriend? Jackie, is it not?"

"I've told you everything. Actually, she's my ex-girlfriend!"

"When you get to London…"

"*If* I get to London," Shola corrected.

"…I'm sure one of the first things you will do is to go and visit her. Let me tell you, there is something about ex-girlfriends, it's similar to when a boxer wants to retire, you want to leave the past alone but you keep coming back, wanting to go out with a big bang!"

Shola had to make an effort not to laugh.

"Alright, you don't want to talk about your girlfriend. Ask me what I will do when I get to France."

Shola smiled and, in the darkness, could feel the warmth of Kapo smiling back.

"What are you going to do in France?"

"I have a friend there, we grew up together in the city. He lives in a place called Nice, which I imagine must be a very nice place. Why else would they call it Nice? Anyway, Nice is near Monaco. I have heard so much about the casinos in Monaco, I hope to cure myself of gambling there."

Shola couldn't help but laugh. Kapo chuckled along with him.

"You hope to gamble 'til you are tired of gambling. Is that what you mean?"

"You know that kind of thing," Kapo conceded.

"Is that your only mission?"

"What else is there to do? I once lived in Belgium for six months. Believe me, I know about boredom. Europe is not the place for me. Give me America any day."

"Why don't you stowaway on a ship heading to America then?"

"How many ships have you seen sailing to America in all the African docks you have been to?"

Shola thought for a while.

"I can't think of any. But maybe that's because I was not looking to go there."

"Me, I have been looking to go there and, I can assure you, there are very few ships that have sailed from Gabon to America in my lifetime. And the security on those few ships. Hmmn! I feel sorry for the mother of the person who is discovered on board one of those ships."

"What do you think would happen if they discovered a stowaway?"

"It is not what I think will happen, my brother. It is the accounts that have reached my ears first hand."

Shola smiled and braced himself for a good story. Kapo launched into one without hesitation. He told Shola how a friend of his had bravely gone where none of them had dared to go before.

He had boarded a ship destined for America, all by himself. Two months later when he returned to Africa he was a broken man, a mere shadow of his former self. He told told Kapo a horror story of the severe beatings he endured each day of his journey at the hands of a sadistic captain who did not consider him a fellow human being. Kapo's friend had given him a blow by blow account of how he was made to work from sun on the horizon in the east to sun on the horizon in the west.

He said that although most of the crew were nice to him and he was given plenty to eat, however it did not encourage the captain to stop the beatings or the verbal abuse.

"Where is your friend now?" Shola asked, intrigued.

"In America."

"How come?"

"Just like you, he didn't give up. He hadn't spent a month at home before crossing to Liberia to steal another boat. He now lives in New York."

"Is that really where you want to go?" Shola queried.

"My brother, does a beggar have a choice?"

"You're quite right, y'know," Shola agreed, "we are beggars. Right now, I feel lower than a beggar. I feel as if every ounce of dignity has been taken from me. I wish I could have simply boarded a plane to London like everyone else."

"We both know why you couldn't. As our African elders say: all fingers are not equal. Let me inform you, many great Africans have had to resort to this same route that we are taking."

"Like who?" Shola challenged with undisguised scepticism.

"Good question. You have heard of Kwame Nkrumah, yes? The first Ghanaian premier, he once stole a ship from Accra to Lagos."

"Are you sure?"

"Would I lie to you. Not only that. You have heard of Nnamdi Azikiwe. The Great Zik, first president of Nigeria. He stowed away from Lagos to America."

"When was this?"

"You are asking me. Am I a historian? It was sometime before he returned to Nigeria to start a political career. So, you see, this might be a sign of great things to come for both of us."

"Fat chance. I haven't the slightest interest in politics."

"Let me tell you, whenever I am on board a ship as a stowaway, do you know what I always think of? I think of how I am so lucky to be on this journey of my own free will."

"And what does that mean?"

"That means I remember those among my forefathers who made this journey long before me, chained and squashed together like sardines, against their free will."

"You mean slavery."

"I mean, think of it for a moment, if you think we are suffering. How do you think they felt on their journey? What do you think they were thinking of? Can you imagine the terror in their eyes, not knowing their destiny or whether they would ever see their loved ones again."

Shola and Kapo fell silent for a long moment while they both cast their minds back to their individual images of slavery. All Shola could remember were scenes from the TV series *Roots.* He remembered vaguely the brief history classes on slavery and its abolition in junior school. Now that he thought about it, he had deliberately not discussed slavery in class. It was all too painful, too shameful and the thought of it made him cringe. If he now felt humiliated, he imagined that those who went bound in chains centuries before him must have felt even worse.

Shola made a mental note to find out more about slavery as soon as he got out of his present predicament.

His mind drifted to the lyrics of a song written by Fela Kuti, the great Nigerian musician. Shola had previously mimed the lyrics without considering its deeper meaning. The song was titled *MASS — Movement Against Second Slavery.* Shola wondered at the reasons that compelled people to leave the land of their ancestors to migrate to a foreign land in search of their dreams. In a way, he and Kapo, like so many others, were not making their way to the Northern Hemisphere of their own free will. They were caught up in a cycle of economic survival and the push to leave the poorer nations, created by the pull from the concentration of wealth among a few countries north of the Equator. Many of those fleeing from the oppression at home would return empty-handed, their dreams unfulfilled, having cleaned the streets but not having achieved much else. So little return for so much hope and ambition. Maybe there was truth in the traditional saying, 'Hard labour does not necessarily lead to wealth, to work like a slave can result in naught'.

Shola and Kapo both remained engrossed in their own thoughts. The silence stretched out until Kapo broke into song, to lift their sinking spirits.

Something inside so strong,

I know that I can make it…

The words of the song seemed to lift them. Shola joined Kapo on the next chorus, clicking his fingers in time. Their hearts were warm with hope, their spirits soaring to the sky in comradeship.

Then they heard footsteps above the container.

"Shhh!" Shola hissed urgently.

They waited, the air in the container thick with anxiety. They heard more footsteps.

"They know we are here. Why are they prolonging the agony?" Shola whispered.

"Maybe not. Easy."

Again, they waited. After what seemed like an unbearable duration, they heard someone outside the container's doors, fiddling with the lock. Then the left door swung open.

Fresh sea air rushed inside the container.

Perched precariously outside was an African man, hanging upside down from the roof of the container. With a wistful grunt he swung himself inside.

Kapo grabbed hold of the man's hand to steady him. Then Kapo looked past him and realised for the first time that their container had been stacked high on top of two other containers. A fall could be fatal.

Shola leaned forward and pulled the container door to, leaving just a slight gap open to allow enough moonlight for them to see who their unexpected visitor was.

"You speak English?" Kapo asked.

The man nodded his head, and held up his hand for more time to recover.

"I tell you, they are killers. Murderers!"

The air suddenly turned cold. Shola was filled with a feeling of dread. He knew that he didn't want to hear what was about to be said.

"They killed Rufus! They killed him. For nothing."

"Who killed Rufus?" asked Kapo anxiously.

"Can you believe it? Just like that. Oh my God!"

"What's your name?" Kapo asked, calming him.

"Joseph."

"Where did you and Rufus board this ship?"

"Sierra Leone. Ahhh! Had I known...!"

"Did you see them kill Rufus?" continued Kapo.

Joseph nodded his head. Before shaking it ruefully.

"Who killed him? Was it one of the crew?" queried Shola anxiously, moving closer.

"How am I to know?" Joseph wailed. "It was a man. The others watched him hit Rufus. He hit him, hit him, hit him, then threw him overboard. Bam! Finished! Ohhhh...!"

An uneasy feeling of fear came over both Shola and Kapo. They fell silent for a while. Joseph continued to groan, shaking his head. Kapo stood shaking, unable to talk. Shola kneeled, his head on the floor of the container. He closed his eyes tightly, wishing to wake up in a warm, safe place far away from the present.

He sat up and searched feverishly inside his shirt pocket for a cigarette. He lit one, the flame from his cheap lighter illuminating the nervousness on his face. As he smoked the cigarette, Shola slowly massaged his forehead and temples.

"Kapo. We need to think... carefully?" Shola said finally.

"What is there to think about? Rufus is dead!" rebuked Joseph.

"Yes, Joseph. Rufus is dead..." Shola took a deep breath, "but we have to think of ourselves and how we can stay alive. Who are these people. Are they criminals? What will they do if they find us? Will they kill us too?"

There were more questions than answers. Kapo had a couple of his own.

"Do they know we are here? Did they see you?" he asked.

Joseph nodded.

"Then they must be looking for you."

"Where are we now? How long before we reach the next port?" Shola asked.

Two blank stares answered his question.

"All I know is that at some stage the ship is due to dock in France," stated Kapo.

"We must change our hiding place. They are looking for Joseph. They are bound to search the containers eventually."

"Where can we hide?" asked Kapo.

"Anywhere. Some other place, just as safe."

"You are right, you know," said Kapo. "Should they notice the container doors are unlocked, they will know we are here."

"My friends," Joseph addressed them, "they are looking for me. There is no need for you to be involved. I will go back out. I will give myself up. That is what I will do," he said, rising to his feet.

"Never! I say no. No way! We came as two, now we are three. Wherever we go, we will go together," assured Kapo.

Shola looked on. Surely he was dreaming all this. Soon the curtains would fall and he would wake up for the final bow.

Roget had now not slept for thirty-six hours, the adrenaline of the search keeping him awake. Search? For him it was more like a deer hunt. In his mind, it was 1964 and he was back in Stanleyville as a mercenary fighting for the Congolese National Army against the communist rebels who had taken over one hundred Europeans and Americans hostage. Only this time, the enemy was on his territory. To Roget, the other stowaway remained between him and the captaincy of the *Azuero Reefer.* It was as simple as that. He had to be found and dealt with. And if there were any other stowaways on board, well, woe betide them also.

Roget was in his cabin briefly, catching up on some long overdue rest. He lay with his back on the bunk, smoking and eating fresh fruit. He had taken out the old 9mm automatic he always kept in his kit bag when he sailed, and had loaded it with a clip of bullets. It was his pride and joy, a memento of his days as a mercenary.

He locked his cabin door, before settling back at the table to clean and oil his beloved firearm. Then rummaging deeper in the bag he found the three bullets he was looking for.

They had rigged extra lights into all three holds. Having searched holds number two and three, Captain Wall, Roget and Blondie moved on to number one with the dog.

Captain Wall knew his vessel from bow to stern, from keel to topmast. He had listed in his head the likely places he thought the other stowaway might hide. He was loathe to lead the search, but neither did he want any other members of the crew to be witness to the eventual outcome. It was too late to turn back now, he was in this thing too deep. He had to find the other stowaway to protect himself. But everything had to go smoothly, it was already becoming a little too messy for his liking.

Roget followed the captain down into the hold. Blondie took up the rear with the Alsatian dog straining at his leash.

It took the dog only seconds to find the hiding place behind some crates of cargo, from which emerged not one, not two, but three Africans. The frightened stowaways stood one behind the other, backing away from the growling dog.

Suddenly, a gun appeared in Roget's hand. The captain shouted "Stop!" At the same time, the tallest of the stowaways made a leap for the gun and it went off with a loud bang which seemed to echo in the hold for ages. The African fell back, eyes glazed over. Dead.

The captain stood paralysed, just staring at Roget who turned to him and simply shrugged his shoulders. The two remaining stowaways made their move in that very instance. They rushed Roget simultaneously, knocking him back so violently that the gun went off with a deafening explosion. In the ensuing struggle, the gun was fired twice more. Each time with fatal consequences.

For a moment, the only human sound was that of Captain Wall moaning. He had been hit by a stray bullet and had blood streaming down his arm. Roget lay underneath one of the stowaways, who had fallen on top of him with a bullet between his eyes.

Roget pushed the dead body off and lifted himself up. All around him was carnage. Two Africans lay dead. The ship's dog had also caught a stray bullet and was lifeless on the floor. And the captain was screaming with the pain of his wound.

The commotion had attracted several of the crew from their cabins onto the main deck. It was only then that Roget realised in panic that one of the stowaways had managed to get away and that his beloved 9mm automatic, was loaded and missing.

Only a few whispered words had passed between Shola, Kapo and Joseph as they huddled together. The mood in the lifeboat, their new hiding place, was sombre. They had heard the gun shots too.

MANHUNT

The captain raised his good arm for attention. The murmurs of the crew gathered on the main deck died down. The sea calmed, and it seemed even the wind quietened to hear him speak.

"I know you have all heard gun shots. Yes, there have been shots fired. And there have been casualties. As you can see I am one of them." The captain paused to catch his breath and looked across at Roget. "We have pirates on board. Three of the them are now dead. But there is at least one more on the ship and there may be others. We shall flush them all out, but be careful, they are armed and extremely dangerous."

The captain paused again, wincing at the pain in his arm. He wanted to lead by example, but could not continue and had to be escorted to his cabin, leaving Roget to organise the men into a search party.

* * *

"What do you think is happening?" Kapo whispered. "We are in big trouble now."

"That's a fucking understatement," Shola snapped with frustration.

"Did you hear them? They called us pirates."

"Which pirates?" Joseph hissed. "So, to stowaway is now the same thing as being a pirate. Was Rufus a pirate? Am I? Look, there were many of us who tried to steal this ship. Myself and Rufus made it. And now the crew need an excuse for killing us, so they are calling us pirates. Those men are killers. Did I not tell you?"

"How do we know that *they* are not pirates?" Kapo wondered aloud.

"There were at least seven stowaways on board," Shola said. "No wonder they're pissed off. It's probably cheaper to kill us all."

"Stop it. Don't talk like that," Kapo rebuked, to allay his own fears. "Never say such a thing…"

"Let's not hide from the truth here. Shit is shit and the Pope is catholic. I'm calling it as I see it. But seriously, we need to escape. I don't want to die. I'm too young to die." Shola's voice vibrated with fear.

"Let me see," Kapo began, "by now the ship should be passing near north Africa. The first European port of call for most of these ships is Las Palmas, or the Spanish mainland. We only have to lie low for a few more days and, as they say, we'll be home and dry."

"A few days!" Shola gasped.

"Maybe two, who knows, it could be four. Whatever the case, we have no choice but to stay here until we reach a port, before trying to escape and reporting the crew to the authorities."

"What if they find us first? And even if they don't, can we survive on the little water we have left?"

"I don't know. But if we continue to sip the water, it should last for another day. After that, well..."

"Well?" Joseph chimed, insisting that Kapo complete the sentence. "Well? We shall be thrown overboard like the rest of them. Don't be afraid to say it. They will shoot us all and throw us to the sharks."

"Speak for yourself. I'm not gonna let no one throw me overboard without putting up a fight," said Shola trying to muster some confidence.

"What will you fight with? Bare hands against their guns? Don't make me laugh," Joseph continued derisively. "They are evil. Devils. They killed Rufus for no reason. Ah, can you believe it?!"

Joseph's sighing grew distant as Shola lapsed into his own thoughts. It suddenly occurred to him that no one, not in Nigeria or anywhere else, knew he was on board the ship. The thought left him cold. If he were not to make it, nobody would ever know what had become of him.

Shola thought of the agony his disappearance would bring to his family. His sisters would grow up knowing that they once had a brother, uncertain of whether he was dead or alive. They would live in hope for that miraculous moment when he would walk through the door. A day that would never dawn, a hollow dream never to be fulfilled.

His thoughts raced to Jackie far away in London. Suddenly he longed to see her. How he now wished he had stayed in England all along and tried to make their relationship work. It was the nearest he had felt to love. If only he had another chance.

Shola's thoughts grew more morbid, all he could think of was death. He wanted to get Kapo and Joseph to promise to get word back to his family were he to die.

Then it occurred to him: What if none of them made it? What would happen then?

Shola tried to break his chain of thought. He tried to think positive. His mission was to get to London, and get to London he would. He had plans for his future and perishing at sea was not among them. Over and over he told himself, "I will survive, I will survive... I will survive." The more he repeated the phrase, the more he believed it.

He brushed the tears from his eyes. He wished he had never seen a ship in his life. He wished the nightmare would somehow end.

But a voice kept whispering in his head: survival.

As he lay there, Shola composed in his head a letter that he wished he could send to Jackie.

Jackie, my love,
I am at last on my journey back home.

As I write these words, I lie hidden in a confined space with my new-found friend Kapo, I will tell you all about him when I get home.

We have had to conceal ourselves in a lifeboat, it's dark, dank and boring but anything will do as long as it gets me where I want to be, next to you, where I belong. The conditions that I have to endure at present are far from satisfactory but when I think of being with you again, it keeps me going.

Jackie, I know I have not been the perfect partner, but I have changed. I have learned to value your love, your friendship and know how lucky I am to have you.
Love Shola xxx

Wall lay on his bunk, staring out of the porthole as the first rays of light dawned on the horizon, wondering if he had done the right thing by putting his chief officer in charge of the ship and whether that would resolve or further exacerbate the situation. But his gunshot wound was causing him too much pain for him to captain the *Azuero Reefer* competently. He wouldn't feel too competent about anything for the next forty-eight hours, until they docked in Gibraltar where he could receive the best in medical treatment.

At the end of the day, Roget was probably the best man to deal with the situation, the captain concluded. After all, these African stowaways were becoming bolder by the day. They were parasites threatening international trade and livelihoods. He had no choice but to make sure that his ship was stowaway-free when they docked back in Europe. Every ship's captain knew that European ports were now fining the shipping companies heavily for every stowaway on board. It wasn't his fault, Wall concluded, that he had to deal harshly with these unwanted passengers. It was him or them. He would lose his job if the shipping company was fined. He had a family to feed. He couldn't allow a stowaway to wreck his career. The buck had been passed down to him to do the dirty work. It had been passed down from the shipping companies, his employers. And the shipping companies in their turn had been forced to do the dirty work of the governments who felt that they had to protect their countries from a steady flow of economic migrants from the poorer nations. It was all about money, Wall decided. At the end of the day, he was just another pawn in the game.

The daybreak seemed to ease his troubled

mind. It had been a long night. It had left him depleted and in need of a long rest. Wall's head dropped onto his shoulders and he fell soundly asleep.

"This is my jungle. No one can hide from me." Roger admired himself in his cabin mirror. The large revolver sitting in its holster at his waist, made him look even more menacing. He had lost his favourite gun but, luckily for him, he always carried a spare weapon in his kitbag.

He left the cabin, his eyes twinkling with malice.

Up on deck, the voices of the restless crew, gathered for the manhunt. Roget was determined to search every nook and cranny on the vessel. He had collected the keys to the safe from the Captain, where he found two handguns and a box of bullets.

"Remember men, take extreme caution. We are hunting desperate men, and they are armed. They won't hesitate to kill us, so if necessary, we must kill them first."

The dozen crew members were split into two groups of six, one led by Blondie the other by Roget. One leading to the hull, the other to the stern of the ship.

The search had been on for several hours. Roget and his group had worked their way through the accommodation quarters. Blondie's group were systematically searching through the containers one at a time.

Shola and Kapo could feel the tension emanating from the deck below as the excited crew continued their manhunt.

"They're just below us," Shola whispered.

Kapo nodded wearily. Their lack of water and heightened anxiety was beginning to take its toll. Joseph roused slowly in the corner. Shola put his index finger in front of his lips to keep him quiet.

On deck, every man in Blondie's team maintained a deathly hush, their eyes looking in the direction of the lifeboat above their heads. Blondie thought that he saw the boat sway. Without saying a word, he signalled for a member of the crew to slowly winch the boat down towards the deck. Moments later the lifeboat started its gradual descent.

Shola, huddled against Joseph, cast a questioning look across at Kapo. He saw Kapo's ghosted stare in the murky light afforded in the lifeboat. He also felt Joseph's body stiffen as their hiding place descended slowly.

Shola's mind was screaming 'stop'. This bad dream had been going on for too long. This was the point where all bad dreams came to an end and you woke up. The pounding of his heart was beginning to choke him, causing him to hyperventilate. He held his mouth open to draw in more air. He closed his eyes to pray, but no coherent words would form in his mind.

Then he felt the boat come to an abrupt halt. He closed his eyes but they fluttered uncontrollably. He sought comfort in those around him. But Kapo seemed to be in a trance, he stared blankly, his lips mumbling in prayer.

Blondie eased the gun from inside the waist of his jeans. Slowly he slipped off the catch. Now the lifeboat was on deck. Two members of the crew unfastened the clips that held the cover over the lifeboat. Blondie stood crouched over the boat like an outlaw gunslinger, one arm in his belt hook, with his gun hand at full stretch. He gave the signal to throw back the cover.

The sun blinded the three stowaways. The double explosion of gunfire brought a convulsive cry from Joseph. Shola's world spun out of control.

CAPTURED

Roget marched along the deck, before the three crew members dragging the leaden weight of the wounded African. Behind them, a trail of blood marked their route.

It was a stroke of luck that he had spotted the African sneaking across the deck, while all other eyes were focused on Blondie and the lifeboat. The chief officer simply took aim, steadied his hand and fired. No need for a warning call to stop and surrender, this wasn't the police force after all.

The sun drifted behind a large cloud and, for a moment, the sky turned dark and moody. Roget felt a tinge of ruefulness as he gathered his thoughts.

He had enjoyed the excitement of the last few days. It was a reminder of how much satisfaction his brief action in the Congo jungle had given him. The danger and the rush of adrenaline were addictive. He wanted more and he wanted it soon.

The crew, however, were already muttering their unease about the situation. They didn't like the Africans any more than their chief officer did. But they were not murderers.

Well, he would do it without them. He and Blondie would dispose of them one by one, throw them overboard and then he would cover his tracks.

The loss of life didn't trouble Roget at all. As far as he was concerned, all Africans were savages and they deserved to be treated like such. He would not rest until the last African stowaway was captured and his 9mm automatic retrieved.

Once again the sun sailed into a dark cloud. Only this time its rays remained extinguished for the duration and day resembled night.

The clouded sky never gave way to the sunshine again that day. The only window that looked onto the outside world wore an unsmiling black face.

Shola turned his head away from the dying man as the door slammed shut. The smell of death and the fear of dying hung in the air of the tiny hold where they were being held captive. It reminded Shola of the local abattoir, a few streets from Papa DaCosta's house in Yaba. The flowing red river from the dead cows and the squeals of the pigs which were about to be slaughtered was sickening.

The last few minutes had been the scariest of Shola's life.

By the time the cover of the lifeboat had been thrown off, Shola was a nervous wreck. As the two gunshots exploded in the air, Shola closed his eyes and braced himself for the impact. Shola waited.

And he waited.

He waited for a bullet that would never come. It felt like an hour of waiting. Sweat streamed from every pore on his body. Joseph, meanwhile, had wet his pants and, as he felt the warm wet trickle run down his trouser leg, Shola thought that he was the culprit, because wetting his pants was exactly what he felt like doing.

Shola breathed a sigh of relief when he opened his eyes and saw Blondie's evil eyes staring back at him. Blondie beckoned that they step out slowly. Shola sat up. He was alive. Kapo was alive, so was Joseph. An incredible relief of tension produced a zipping fart from Kapo. If not for their precarious situation, it would have been embarrassing.

The crew bundled them out of the lifeboat unceremoniously and threw them into a tiny hold, which seemed to double as a punishment hole.

Now they had thrown this youth peppered with bullets in with them, as if they expected him to die there.

The injured youth's moaning was almost too

much to bear. Shola closed his eyes, and his heart jerked with an intense feeling of sorrow. He felt the youth would have been better off being put out of his misery with another bullet. Solemnly, he prayed. He recounted the number of times he had watched films of people waiting to be executed in prison. How the priest came along to render the last rites. Shola wished he now had the opportunity for such a luxury, but this wasn't a film he was in. This was real life, and there were no oscars in real life.

Sitting there, as life slowly ebb from the mortally wounded stowaway, Shola wished he could turn back the hands of time. Kapo was kneeling over the African, whispering words of encouragement with little conviction.

It now appeared to Shola that death would be his constant companion. How he wished he had never brought up the idea of having a send-off party for Jackie and her friends at the University of Lagos. How he wished his father had been as influential as Abi's father, who appeared to smooth things over by waving his magic wallet and through liaison with his high powered connections. Shola wondered if, perhaps, his present ordeal was payback for his part in Kate's death.

Joseph tried communicating with his fellow countryman. The wounded youth could barely speak in a painful groan. Joseph was able to confirm that their friend in common, Mackreal, was dead. So was the wounded youth's elder brother. Only one member of the group that came on board with him was still unaccounted for.

It became too much for Joseph to bear. Mackreal had been a likeable, well-known character around the port area of Freetown. Joseph retired to a corner of the hold, a haunted man.

The dying youth coughed. A dry raspy cough. His chest heaved like he was about to vomit. The next moment he was dead. A dream of a brighter future, extinguished.

For a moment, there was silence amongst the three surviving stowaways. The air was thick with mourning. Joseph began a low moan in the corner.

Shola, too, started crying.

"Do you know why we will survive?" Kapo asked, trying to comfort both his companions. "Because our recently departed friend's spirit will be with us. Until he receives a decent burial, the evil of these sailors' ways will visit their families for ten generations to come!" he cursed through trembling lips. "For now, though, we have to think of ourselves. We have to think of our next move, otherwise we will all become shark food."

For a while nothing was said. Each person held onto their own thoughts. Kapo sensed that his companions were losing faith. Without belief in themselves they would remain at the mercy of their captors.

"Shola! Joseph!" Kapo called. "We are not the

first people to have been in a life or death situation. And we will not be the last." He paused for effect. "Let me tell you guys something, we can live together or we can die together. The choice is yours."

"What the hell are you talking about?" Shola responded in frustration.

"Hey, Shola, do you know if it weren't for you I wouldn't be here now," Kapo said.

"So what? You blaming me for all of this?"

"Who else? Unless I blame Joseph."

"Then am I to blame for them killing Rufus? Am I to blame for them killing Mackreal and the others?" Joseph said.

"Who told you to steal this ship?" demanded Kapo.

"Me?" asked Joseph indignantly.

"Yes, you. You! Why did you steal this ship?"

"What about you? Is this your ship? Are you the owner?" Joseph asked angrily.

"Kapo, you're losing it, mate. What's the use in distressing the guy?"

"It is you who is losing it. Otherwise you would be listening to me for my experience."

"Screw you! And screw your experience. Let your experience get us out of this then."

"You want to screw me and my experience?" Kapo said. "Come on then, screw me. Here I am."

Shola suddenly felt stupid, he relaxed his guard and afforded himself a smile. A moment before he was feeling downheartened and had almost given up the will to fight. Now, he was ready to take on all comers.

"Don't you feel better when you can be angry?" Kapo said. "Anger makes you want to live. Come, let us plan."

In his dream, Roget motioned to his soldiers to tread softly and remain quiet. Soon they arrived at the clearing. Peering through the drooping banana leaves he could see the captain struggling to free himself from the skewer he was tied to, as the flames crept higher. The cries and yelps of the bloodlusting natives surrounding the fire sickened him to the stomach.

At a sign from Roget, the soldiers rushed into the clearing to engage the natives in battle. Roget led by example, both revolvers blazing. Amidst the confusion and fighting, the screams of the captain pierced the air as the flames singed him.

Roget got to him first and saved the captain in the nick of time. He was a hero, only the captain held him responsible for his brush with death and refused to recommend him for a decoration. Instead, he attempted to have his rescuer court martialed for desertion.

Roget's dream was interrupted by the presence of someone in his cabin. Startled, he opened his eyes to see one of the crew who worked in the ship's kitchen standing over him.

"What are you doing in my room?" Roget demanded.

"I've come to speak with you, so that you

don't dig yourself into deeper trouble. I've seen enough blood for one lifetime."

"Get out!"

"Roget, listen to me. You are in desperate need of help. If only the captain could see you now. He wouldn't..."

"Get out! That's an order," shouted Roget swinging his feet from the bunk. He couldn't believe the man's insubordination.

"Don't for one moment, think that you are going to get away with this."

The crewman eased open the door as Roget lifted himself off his bunk. Roget shoved the intruder in the chest and out of his cabin door.

The crewman picked himself up off the floor outside where he fell. "Don't think I don't know your murderous intention," he hissed. "I want no more part of it."

"Then you'd better find yourself another job when we dock." Roget's blood boiled. "Do you know who pays your wage? It's not these illegal Africans, it's the shipping company. You ought to remind yourself of that. Speak to your fellow crewmen and I think you'll find, they know which side their bread is buttered. We're all in this together."

"That's still no reason to resort to murder."

Roget smiled sickly. "Do you really think for one minute that Europe really wants to be swamped by these vermin? They'll probably give me a medal for what I've done!"

With that, Roget slammed his cabin door and

returned to his bunk.

The *Azuero Reefer* rose and fell swiftly, which had a soothing effect on the crewman's jangled nerves as he stood on the open deck. The revulsion he felt still persisted, but there was a speck of truth in Roget's murderous ranting.

The crew were predominantly from the independent states of the former Soviet Union, providing highly skilled, cheap labour. But with the added burden of 'carrier liability', each stowaway threatened the livelihood of every member of the crew. Roget knew they had little choice but to comply with his evil mission.

Inside his cabin, Roget poured himself another straight whisky. For a while he sat there, shaking with rage. Finally, he decided it was time. He would go and get Blondie and several others in the crew, together they would drag the stowaways out of the hold one at a time and dispose of them. None of them would ever see dry land again. He would not waste any more time.

TIME FOR ACTION

Shola and Kapo huddled together for warmth in the tiny hold. It was freezing. Kapo was sure that they were fast approaching the European continent for the weather to have changed so drastically within the last twenty-four hours.

"Hey, Kapo, when do we put our plan into action?" asked Shola, feeling ready to take on the world.

"When they come for us."

"When's that likely to be?"

But Kapo's guess was as good as Shola's. One thing for sure, the crew had to come and deal with them before they docked in Europe. And that wouldn't be too long now.

They had decided to take the initiative. They figured that they were only being kept alive until the last elusive stowaway was captured. While one stowaway remained at liberty to tell the tale, the crew could not carry out their ultimate aim of disposing of all the Africans. Whilst that one stowaway eluded his pursuers, Kapo, Joseph and Shola could expect to be kept alive.

But surely one man could not remain elusive on a ship indefinitely. In which case, they would have to prepare themselves for the moment when they would be faced with the same fate that had befallen their dead comrades. There were three of them. When the crew came for them, they would have to rush them, despite their weapons. The element of surprise was on their side, if they could only seize one of the weapons or a member of the crew to use as a shield, they might still be able to survive. Of course, they might not all make it. That was the reality. But they had to go out fighting, and if just one of them made it, it would have been worth it.

At first Joseph was not too happy with Kapo's plan. He would have preferred begging for their lives, appealing to the crew's human kindness. Kapo had to laugh. He reminded Joseph that the crew were already in this thing too deep.

"Why would they want us to remain alive as witnesses to all their murders, out of the goodness of their heart? My friend, you know that that is not a realistic option. In this situation, attack is the best method of defence," Kapo said. "It is our only chance of leaving this ship alive."

Shola agreed and, eventually, so did Joseph.

"If we capture one of them, we can demand to be set free," Kapo continued.

"Set free to where? Into the bottom of the sea?" Joseph offered.

"This is the only way they will listen to us. What have we to lose?"

"We could lose our lives for a start!"

"At least this way we too will kill one or two of the bastards before they kill us."

"No one's killing me! I'm not ready to die!" Shola stated hoarsely, a lump forming in his throat.

"If we have to die, we have to die," Kapo reasoned, "but my soul will rest in peace if only one of us is able to make it alive to testify against these evil murderers. Whichever one of us comes out of this alive must promise the others to pursue these men until the ends of the earth to get justice."

"Remember, every man for himself," Joseph swore solemnly.

"And God for us all," Kapo offered in prayer.

At that moment, they heard the sound of the latch above their heads opening. Each man braced themselves, ready. This was it.

"My brothers..." A voice called out to them from above.

They looked up to see the dark face of a fellow African, smiling down at them.

"Quickly. There is no time to waste."

The three captives did not need to consider their options. They helped each other out of the hold and rushed up on deck for the salty, sea air taste of freedom.

Their rescuer, Valentine, was the last of the stowaways who came on board with Joseph.

More importantly, he had managed to get hold of a weapon, a deadly-looking 9mm automatic.

"At last," Kapo smiled. "God is on our side."

No sooner had he said that however, than the sound of shots rang out in the air. From the other end of the ship, Blondie and Roget came running towards the stowaways, guns blazing.

Valentine managed to fire a couple of rounds back as everybody dived for cover. He was reluctant to fire any more though, because he knew he had to save bullets.

But Roget and Blondie had no such restraints. They continued firing, and moving forward.

The stowaways had no choice but to scramble, each one in a different direction. But Joseph tripped up. Before he was able to scramble to his feet, Roget was on top of him with his gun at his head.

As he ran, Shola heard Joseph call out his name. He turned his head and saw the two crewmen throw him overboard.

Now Shola's heart started beating fast. There was nothing he could do for Joseph. He had to think of himself. He moved with speed and stealth along the deck, looking for sanctuary. Shola's main thought was to get as far away from the crewmen's rage as was possible.

Shola tried to think of a place to hide but his mind remained blank. He saw the face of death before him. A shiver ran through him, once, then again.

The stormy sea tilted the ship first one way,

then the other. The waves lashed harder and harder, with each one curling higher than the previous. The spray from the waves spilled onto the deck as the wind began to pick up in speed, making the deck precarious for all who were not down below.

Shola knew he had to act, and act fast.

For a moment he looked at the dark rising waves. He wondered whether to jump into the sea and perish in the watery grave was an easier option than dying by a bullet to the head.

He tried to bring his mind back to the task at hand, but the scenes he had just witnessed kept flashing through his mind. Shola listened. He thought he had heard a footstep. He was mistaken, it was the howling wind playing tricks with his mind.

Eventually, he had found himself in the noisy but empty engine room below deck. But he knew he couldn't hide there indefinitely. If the crew were to search the engine room, he would be trapped.

A half bottle of whisky, left there by one of the crew gave him an idea. He still had his cheap plastic lighter on him. If Kapo was right, and they were close to Europe, what better way was there to call for help but to start a fire. The Mediterranean was one of the busiest sea routes in the world. Which meant if he could raise the alarm, there was every chance a ship would come to their aid.

* * *

It had all happened so fast. Amidst all the commotion coming from the deck, Kapo raced across the tops of the containers trying to keep some distance between him and his two pursuers. He kept running and hoping that there was a way out for him. Suddenly he stopped dead in his tracks. Blocking his route was a crew member wielding an iron bar.

The sailor paused for a second before rushing towards Kapo. Kapo was ready for him. He ducked the swinging bar. The sailor lost his footing and fell.

But now the two who were chasing him had caught up. One made a lunge for the stowaway, but Kapo side stepped the sailor's outstretched hands. The other sailor aimed a looping right to his head. Kapo took the blow on his shoulder, then leapt up and went flying, feet first into his chest. He wasted no time in unleashing a flurry of karate kicks to the man's head and groin. The sailor gripped onto him, his face a mask of pain, as he fell to his knees.

Just when he thought he was going to get away, Kapo felt a stinging blow from the iron bar to his ankles. It was painful to say the least and he felt sure that he had broken a bone in the leg. Now the sailor was back on top, ready to swing his weapon down on the stowaway's head. In desperation Kapo lashed out with his uninjured leg, sweeping his assailant's leg from beneath him. The sailor dropped beside him with a heavy thud.

The sailor swung the iron bar. Kapo threw his head back, just out of reach. But the second blow didn't miss. The sailor brought the metal bar crashing down on the side of Kapo's face. The African dropped like a ninepin.

With the help of another member of the crew, the sailor dragged Kapo's lifeless body to the edge of the boat and threw the African over the side.

It had been a hot gunbattle. Valentine was on the bridge, cornered. He had fired his last shot. Now Blondie and Roget stepped out from their firing positions, and made their way onto the bridge slowly. On seeing them, Valentine's eyes widened with terror. As Roget took aim, Valentine threw the 9mm automatic at him. That was the last thing he did in this life. The force of the shot from Blondie's gun threw him back, leaving him with a deep wound in his chest. A wide grin spread across Roget's face. Now they would deal with the last stowaway.

Shola looked up at the sky as if questioning the wisdom of the one above. The rain pelted him, causing him to blink continuously. He looked away to the horizon. Somewhere far away across the vast stretch of sea he saw lights, reaching out to him, sowing a seed of hope in his determination.

He thought back to the day he had been introduced to Mohammed. How they had walked along the docks to a quiet spot before he had parted with his money. He pictured himself how he had stood by the dock that day, looking out to the bluish-grey sea and the ships sailing on it. Little did he know what was in store. Not for one moment did he think he would be in a situation like this.

The fire was blazing now in the engine room. There was confusion on deck as members of the crew rushed to try and put out the flames. But their extinguishers were useless against the thick grey smoke that billowed towards them.

From his new hiding place high up at the top of the ship's mast, Shola looked down on the chaos down below and prayed that none of the crew would look skywards. From his vantage point he could see far out on the horizon, two ships change their course and head towards the blazing inferno of the *Azuero Reefer*.

It was only a matter of time now.

HELL ON EARTH

The guilt of being the only one left of seven hopefuls who had sought a passage to a new life rested heavy on him. The thought of having a duty to the others partly assuaged the guilt Shola felt at being the sole survivor. It emboldened him, suppressing his fear. His heart filled with determination to see the crew of the *Azuero Reefer* behind bars. He had been through too much to not see it through to its end. His life had been spared for a reason, the most obvious reason was to see that his friends received justice. He would also take it upon himself when he returned to London, to make every effort to locate Kapo and Joseph's families from the little information he had gathered during their journey together, to tell them of the sad fate of their loved ones.

The court room was buzzing with lawyers, journalists, diplomats, observers from human rights groups and representatives of the shipping companies. All of them had come to hear the judge's summing up of a case which had captured the imagination of the whole of France, not just because of the specific ugliness of the crime, but for the significance of its motive. The crew of the *Azuero Reefer* sat in the dock awaiting their fate. Watchful, alert, betraying no emotion, eyes scanning the scene before him, an unrepentant Roget glared across the courtroom at the sole surviving stowaway, the one that got away. Even now, the sight of the ship's chief officer was able to fill Shola with terror. Day after day for the last four weeks he had sat in his high-backed wooden chair, in the impressive Cour d'Assises in Rouen, France, facing the men who had tried to kill him, the men who had murdered all his companions.

Shola had told his story to the court. He had given a thorough account of how he came to stow away on board the *Azuero Reefer*, hoping to make it back to England. He told of his friends, Kapo, Joseph, Valentine and their dreams of reaching the West for a chance of a better life from the poverty of life in the slums of West Africa. He told the court about how these young men's lives had been snuffed out one after the other, by a murderous crew led by the chief officer of the ship.

He sat with his head hung low between his knees, his eyes full of tears as his aching heart cried. He had lost Kapo and now he knew how much he had bonded with the man. The man had been everything from a friend and teacher to an older brother, an experience he had never had before.

The presiding judge sat stony-faced as Shola told his story. In all his years in criminal law, even he had not heard a tale of such horror.

"But you should be giving me a medal for what I have done," Roget insisted when it was his turn to take the stand. "Without people like me, these savages would be swarming all over France."

That wasn't the sort of comment that endeared Roget to the judge and when it came time for sentencing, he was given a stiff life sentence.

BRIGHT LIGHTS

Dear Shola,
Just a quick note to let you know that you are now the father of a beautiful baby boy. Oh Shola, he is absolutely gorgeous, a real bundle of joy. Wait until you see him, he's got your exact eyes and your complexion too, and a grin that reminds me of you. The only thing he's got from me is his nose, but I'm happy all the same.

The labour wasn't as hard as I expected it to be but it was hard all the same. I was in labour for around fifteen hours and then they had to induce me as the poor little mite went into foetal distress, his heart rate slowed down, almost stopping. He's a survivor, a warrior.

In my next letter I shall send you a

picture of our wonderful son. But hurry home, he'll be asking for his daddy soon, and then what am I going to tell him?
Love you. Jackie xxx

Shola's uncle welcomed him at the airport. All the way in his car to his new flat in Stratford, he asked question after question of his nephew. Shola could tell he was trying to disguise his concern by keeping the conversation light-hearted.

At the flat, the hot bath and cocoa were followed by more burning questions. Shola was exhausted and so kept the answers concise.

"Wonders shall never cease," his uncle remarked, looking thoughtful. "Your story sounds like a miracle."

Shola nodded in agreement.

"Do you know it's been five months since your father first phoned to say you were missing. And every week since then, despite the cost, your mother has called, blaming herself for not giving you enough money for your travels."

"She tried her best," Shola replied. "Thank God, everything's turned out okay."

Shola smiled as he thought of his parents. He no longer felt any anger towards his father. He promised himself he would write to them soon, since he had undoubtedly contributed more than his fair share of grey to the hair on their heads.

After answering all his uncle's questions, Shola made the call that had been on his mind since his flight touched down. Jackie's mother picked up the phone, surprised to hear his voice.

"She's at her aunt's house," the mother informed him and gave him the address.

Shola spent the rest of the night writing letters to the families of his stowaway companions who had not made it. He hoped his personal account to their loved ones last days would go some way to heal the pain.

The following morning, Shola obtained money from his uncle to pay Jackie a surprise visit at the house in Essex.

He was so looking forward to seeing her, especially to hug her after the horrors of the last few months. And, of course, he couldn't wait to hold the baby boy which her mother told him that Jackie had given birth to.

The house he was looking for was similar to the others on the quiet street. Just as he turned into the driveway, he heard his name being called. His whole body took on a glow and a smile lit his face as he recognised the voice. Jackie waved and disappeared from the window, appearing again seconds later at the front door.

They hugged each other long and hard, before Jackie let go and stood back to look him over.

"What's happened to you. You look like you've been on a hunger strike."

Shola smiled, noticing that she had changed too. Her facial features were flared and he could notice the slight bulge under her blouse. They hugged again and, this time, Shola stole a passionate kiss.

He felt like he'd been granted three of his wishes. He was alive. He was in London. And he was back with Jackie.

But he had just one more wish; to hold his baby.

"I swear he's a gift from God. Where is he? Can I see him?"

Jackie invited him inside the house and took him by the hand into her bedroom, where a sleeping baby was lying in a cot.

Tears came to Shola's eyes as he lifted his baby gently out of the cot and cradled him in his arms. He felt immediately like a father and responsible for the child's well-being. He didn't want to wake his son up now, but he would wait in the house until the baby woke up and got his first glimpse of his father.

Meanwhile, Jackie led him into the living room and after making a cup of tea for them both, sat Shola down to talk.

He told her of what had happened since she left Nigeria. Gave her a blow by blow account of how he had been expelled from university and then found himself destitute and without his passport in Lagos. He told her of both his attempts to stowaway and about his friend Kapo. And then he told her of the murderous crew aboard the *Azuero Reefer*. Needless to say Jackie was horrified. She had read about the account in the newspapers, but hearing it first hand was even more shocking.

"Oh Shola," she said, putting a reassuring arm around him as he recollected the horror of his journey from Africa, "you've been through so much. The difficult pregnancy I went through doesn't seem to compare. For a while I hated you, Shola, for not being there with me. I thought you were having it easy because I was going through the whole thing by myself. It would have been a lot easier if you were here. Well, you're home now and we have to decide. what's going to happen between us. I just want a future... for myself... for him..."

Shola got up and paced the room uneasily.

"I've been doing a lot of thinking in the last few months, I'm not the Shola I was when we last met. I can see things in a new perspective. I'm a lot more responsible now. I know I've been selfish, but all that has changed now. I have learnt a lot of lessons about life."

"Keep talking," Jackie urged.

"I want to be a father to my child. I want us to be together. So, let's get married Jackie."

At first her eyes lit up, taken aback by the proposal. Then the reality of the situation sunk in.

"I wish it was that simple, Shola."

"I know. I know." He sat down beside her and put his arm around her. "There's our relationship, money problems… everything seems so unclear. But if there's one thing you should know, Jackie, it's that I'm willing to commit. I know that we can work things out… for me, for you and for our baby."

"Maybe. I'm just not sure about anything anymore."

Shola could understand that. The two of them sat in silence for a while. Then Jackie looked at him. "I think whatever we do, whatever plans we make, the first thing we should do is give him a name."

"He doesn't have a name?"

"Not a proper one."

"What if we call him… Isaiah."

"Hopefully my father will be overjoyed by this choice and not complain about us being teenage parents!."

Jackie smiled. "I like that."

"Isaiah, it is then!"

BESTSELLING FICTION

I wish to order the following X Press title(s)

Title	Author	Price
❑ Single Black Female	Yvette Richards	£5.99
❑ When A Man Loves A Woman	Patrick Augustus	£5.99
❑ Wicked In Bed	Sheri Campbell	£5.99
❑ Rude Gal	Sheri Campbell	£5.99
❑ Yardie	Victor Headley	£4.99
❑ Excess	Victor Headley	£4.99
❑ Yush!	Victor Headley	£5.99
❑ Fetish	Victor Headley	£5.99
❑ Here Comes the Bride	Victor Headley	£5.99
❑ In Search of Satisfaction	J. California Cooper	£7.99
❑ Sistas On a Vibe	Ijeoma Inyama	£6.99
❑ Flex	Marcia Williams	£6.99
❑ Baby Mother	Andrea Taylor	£6.99
❑ Uptown Heads	R.K. Byers	£5.99
❑ Jamaica Inc.	Tony Sewell	£5.99
❑ Lick Shot	Peter Kalu	£5.99
❑ Professor X	Peter Kalu	£5.99
❑ Obeah	Colin Moone	£5.99
❑ Cop Killer	Donald Gorgon	£4.99
❑ The Harder They Come	Michael Thelwell	£7.99
❑ Baby Father	Patrick Augustus	£6.99
❑ Baby Father 2	Patrick Augustus	£6.99
❑ OPP	Naomi King	£6.99

I enclose a cheque/postal order (Made payable to '*The X Press*') for

£ ________

(add 50p P&P per book for orders under £10. All other orders P&P free.)

NAME ______________________________

ADDRESS ______________________________

____

Cut out or photocopy and send to:
X PRESS, 6 Hoxton Square, London N1 6NU
Alternatively, call the X PRESS hotline: 0171 729 1199 and place your order.

WHEN A MAN LOVES A WOMAN BY PATRICK AUGUSTUS

"One thing's for certain...no man is ever gonna love you the way I do..."

Campbell Clarke grew up poor, whereas Dionne Owen came from a wealthy and respected buppie family. When they met a week before her marriage to City broker Mike Phillips, Campbell knew instantly that Dionne was the woman he wished HE was marrying.
The following years took their lives down very separate roads, but Campbell is prepared to wait as long as it takes to win Dionne's love.

"Excellent...a modern romance that every man and woman can relate to."
The Voice

"A compulsive read...written with humour and a real understanding of the soul of a black man."
Yvette Richards

ISBN 1-874509-24-7

BABY FATHER 2 BY PATRICK AUGUSTUS

"Baby Father...an entertaining look at four black guys on the town who enjoy womanising but suddenly discover the joys of parenthood."
Daily Mirror

When JOHNNY finally decides to spend some quality time with his baby son, he is vexed to find that his parental duties have been taken over by his baby mother's new lover.
Thirtysomething BERES discovers that his new wife's baby father isn't too happy about the recent developments in their domestic arrangements either.
LINVALL'S neglected his role as a father for so long that now, when he's called to play dad, he's long forgotten how to do it!
Eligible bachelor GUSSIE yearns to have kids but he still can't find a woman whose 'rateable market value' is as high as his...AND TO CAP IT ALL, THE WOMEN HAVE GOT THEM UNDER MANNERS!

"A superb follow up to the massive hit novel Baby Father."
Paperbacks Reviewed

"Patrick Augustus writes with a voice that is totally unique. He deserves all the success he's had."
The Voice

ISBN 1-874509-15-8